The Loner:
RATTLESNAKE VALLEY

The Loner:
RATTLESNAKE VALLEY

J. A. Johnstone

PINNACLE BOOKS
Kensington Publishing Corp.
www.kensingtonbooks.com

PINNACLE BOOKS are published by

Kensington Publishing Corp.
119 West 40th Street
New York, NY 10018

All Kensington titles, imprints, and distributed lines are available at special quantity discounts for bulk purchases for sales promotions, premiums, fund-raising, educational, or in-stitutional use. Special book excerpts or customized printings can also be created to fit specific needs. For details, write or phone the office of the Kensington special sales manager: Kensington Publishing Corp., 119 West 40th Street, New York, NY 10018, attn: Special Sales Department; Phone: 1-800-221-2647.

ISBN-13: 978-0-7860-2278-6
ISBN-10: 0-7860-2278-7

First printing: April 2010

10 9 8 7 6 5 4 3 2 1

Printed in the United States of America

Chapter 1

Kid Morgan reined his horse to a halt and looked at the bleached white skull on the ground in front of him. He rested his hands on the saddle horn and leaned forward to study not only the grotesquely grinning skull but also the two long bones laid across each other that accompanied it.

"Skull and crossbones," The Kid muttered. "Pirates."

More than a dozen years earlier, in what seemed like a previous, half-forgotten lifetime ago when he had still been known as Conrad Browning, The Kid had read a novel called *Treasure Island*. He knew about pirates and the symbol on the flags flown on their ships.

The question was, what was that ominous symbol doing in the mostly arid landscape of West Texas, hundreds of miles from the sea?

The Kid lifted his head. Keen eyes gazed at his surroundings. A broad valley bordered by ranges of low, brush-covered hills fell away to his left and right and stretched in front of him for at least twenty miles to the east before the hills closed in sharply and pinched it off, leaving only a narrow opening for the trail. Beyond the hills, what appeared to be an endless stretch of sandy wasteland was visible through the gap. Behind The Kid was the pass through which he had just ridden in the rugged gray mountains that closed off the western end of the valley.

In stark contrast to the desert, the mountains, and the scrubby hills, the valley itself was an unexpected oasis of green. A line of trees marked the meandering course of a river that rose from springs in the mountains and flowed eastward, watering the rangeland on either side of it before the desert wasteland swallowed it whole at the far end of the valley. The grass that covered the range might not have been considered lush in some parts of the world, but in West Texas, it certainly was. Not surprisingly, The Kid saw cattle grazing here and there, hardy longhorns that not only survived but actually thrived on the graze they found. A man who had been riding for days through sandy, rocky country that wasn't much good for anything, as The Kid had, would find the sight of the valley mighty appealing.

Except for the skull and crossed bones in the trail that looked for all the world like a warning to keep out.

A tight smile pulled at the corners of Kid

Morgan's mouth. Even before the events that had changed his life so dramatically, he had never been the sort of hombre who took kindly to being told what to do. He lifted the reins and heeled the buckskin into motion again.

As he did, movement stirred *within* the bleached skull, visible behind the empty eye sockets. A rattlesnake suddenly crawled out through one of those sockets and coiled on the ground. The vicious buzz of its rattles filled the air as it raised its head, ready to strike. Its forked tongue flickered in and out of its mouth.

The Kid's horse was used to gunfire and the smell of powder smoke, but the sound and scent of the snake spooked it. The buckskin tossed its head, shied away, and tried to rear up.

The Kid's strong left hand on the reins kept the horse under firm control. His right hand brushed his black coat aside and dipped to the Colt holstered on his hip. Steel whispered against leather as he drew the gun, then the hot, still air was shattered by the blast of a shot.

It seemed that The Kid hadn't even taken time to aim, but the snake's head exploded as the bullet found it. The thick body with its diamond-shaped markings uncoiled and writhed frenziedly as the knowledge of its death raced through its prehistoric nervous system. The Kid's lips tightened in distaste as he watched the snake whip around and die.

With his gun still in his hand, The Kid dismounted. He stepped around the snake, which had a grisly red smear where its head used to be. A swift kick from The Kid sent the skull bouncing into some brush. He reached down, picked up one of the long bones, and flung it off in a different direction. The other bone went sailing away with another flick of his wrist.

You shouldn't have done that, a voice seemed to say in the back of his head. *Whoever those bones belonged to may have been innocent of any wrongdoing.*

The Kid didn't know if the voice belonged to his own conscience—not that he would have admitted to having such a thing after all the men he had killed, justifiably or not—or to his late wife. Either way, hearing voices was a sure sign that a person was going mad.

The revulsion he had felt toward the snake was the last straw. He'd already been a little angry about being warned to keep out of the valley and he'd given in to his irritation.

He usually tried to keep his emotions under control at all times. A man who wanted to live very long in that harsh land couldn't afford to let himself be distracted by hatred or fear or loneliness.

Morgan was a tall, lean young man, not yet thirty, with sandy hair under a flat-crowned black hat. He wore a dusty black coat over a white shirt, and black trousers that weren't tucked into his high-topped boots. His saddle was a good one, relatively new, and he carried two long guns in sheaths strapped to the horse, a Winchester and a heavy-caliber Sharps. His clothes and gear were a notch above those of the average saddle tramp, but his deeply tanned face and the slight squint around his eyes that was becoming permanent spoke of a man who spent most of his time outdoors.

That hadn't always been the case. Once he had spent his days either in an office or a mansion, depending on whether or not he felt like working. As Conrad Browning, he had grown up among the wealthy on Boston's Beacon Hill, had attended the finest academies and universities, had taken his place in the business world and owned stakes in mines, railroads, and shipping companies. He was rich, with probably more money than he could spend in the rest of his life.

None of that meant a damn thing after his wife was murdered.

He avenged her death by tracking down and killing the men responsible for it, and chose not to return to his old life as the business tycoon Conrad Browning. Instead he held on to the new identity he had created in his quest for vengeance, that of the gunfighter known as Kid Morgan. For months now he had roamed the Southwest, riding alone for the most part, not searching for trouble but not avoiding it when it came to him, as it seemed it inevitably did.

For a while, a young woman he'd met during some trouble in Arizona had traveled with him, but she had stayed behind in Santa Fe to make a new life for herself while he continued drifting eastward into Texas. That was better, The Kid thought. It was easier not to get hurt when you didn't allow anyone to get too close to you.

He was reaching for the buckskin's reins when a voice called, "Don't move, mister!"

Two things made The Kid freeze. One was the tone of command in the voice, which meant it was probably backed up by a gun. The other was surprise that the voice belonged to a woman. He looked over his shoulder and saw her coming out of a nearby clump of boulders. He'd guessed right about the gun. She had a Winchester leveled at him.

"Don't even twitch a muscle," she ordered, "or you'll be damn sorry."

"Take it easy," The Kid began, but the woman didn't. She pulled the trigger and the Winchester went off with a sharp crack.

Just before the shot, though, The Kid heard another wicked buzzing from somewhere very close by. The buckskin jumped and landed running, racing a good twenty yards before it came to a halt. The Kid stayed right where he was, just in case the woman had missed.

She hadn't. When he looked down, he saw a second rattler writhing and jerking in its death throes at his feet. He hadn't seen it slither out from among the rocks bordering the trail, but there it was, and very easily could have sunk its fangs in his leg.

The woman's shot hadn't been quite as clean as The Kid's. Her bullet had ripped away a good chunk of flesh from the snake's body just behind its head, a gaping wound from which crimson blood gushed, but the head was still intact and attached to the body. The mouth was open and ready to bite, and The Kid knew that dying or not, the venom was still there and the creature was as dangerous as ever.

He lifted his foot and brought the heel of his boot crunching down on the snake's head, striking almost as fast and lethally as a snake himself.

He ground his heel back and forth in the dirt, crushing the rattler's head and ending its threat. Then he looked over at the woman, who had lowered the rifle, and said coolly, "Thanks for the warning."

"I shot the blasted thing."

"Yes, but you didn't kill it," The Kid pointed out.

"You know how hard it is to hit the head of a snake when it's moving?"

The Kid smiled and made a casual gesture toward the second reptile carcass that lay on the ground nearby. "Apparently I do," he drawled.

The woman came forward, looked at the snake The Kid had shot, and frowned. "That first shot I heard?"

"Yeah."

She let out a low whistle of admiration. "Pretty good."

The Kid could have said the same thing about her appearance, as well as her shooting. She was in her early twenties, he estimated, with curly golden hair pulled back behind her head. She wore a low-crowned brown hat with its strap taut under her chin. Her skin had a healthy tan a little lighter in shade than her hair. She wore a brown vest over a white shirt and a brown riding skirt and boots. She didn't look like the sidesaddle type.

She still held the Winchester, and while the rifle wasn't pointed at The Kid, she carried it with an easy assurance that said she could swing the barrel toward him again very quickly if she needed to. Keeping her distance, she asked, "Who are you?"

"The name's Morgan," he replied, not offering any more information than that.

"Why'd you kick that skull into the brush? The poor hombre it belonged to never did you any harm."

"I know," he said without mentioning that the same thought had occurred to him. "I took it as a warning to keep out of the valley . . . and I don't like being told where I can and can't go."

"A warning is exactly what it was," she said, "and you were foolish to disregard it. But if you were bound and determined to do that, why didn't you just ride around it?"

"I wanted whoever put it there to know how I felt." He paused and studied her. "Was that you?"

She bristled in anger. The Winchester's muzzle edged toward him as she said, "Do I look like the sort of person who'd do something like that?"

"I don't know," The Kid said. "That's why I

asked. You're the one who just told me I'd be making a big mistake if I rode on into the valley."

"Well, for your information, I *didn't* put those bones there. I'm not the one you have to worry about. It's—"

She stopped short. Her head came up in a listening attitude. Alarm leaped into her eyes.

The Kid heard it, too. A swift rataplan of hoofbeats that was approaching too fast. Half a dozen riders swept around a stand of thick brush about fifty yards away and thundered toward them.

Chapter 2

There was nothing The Kid could do except stand his ground. He had six rounds in his Colt, which meant it was possible to kill all six of the strangers—if he was damn lucky.

But the young woman was armed, too, he reminded himself, and if she could account for one or two of them, he might be able to get the rest. Of course, he would probably die, too, and so would she, but it was better to go down fighting and take as many of your enemies with you as you could.

Maybe it wouldn't come to that, he thought as the riders reined in . . . although from the looks of the bunch, they were no strangers to killing.

The man who sat his horse a little in front of the others was a big hombre, tall and broad shouldered with brawny arms. The sleeves of his blue shirt were rolled up over forearms matted with dark hair. More hair curled from the open throat of the shirt. A beard jutted from his belligerent jaw. A gray hat was cuffed to the back of his head. He wore a pair of pearl-handled revolvers. Cruel, deep-set eyes studied The Kid from sunken pits under bushy eyebrows.

The apparent leader was the biggest of the bunch, but the man who rode to his right was almost as large. His slablike jaw bristled with rusty stubble, and a handlebar mustache of the same shade twisted over his mouth. As he took off the battered old derby he wore and used it to fan away some of the dust that had swirled up from the horses' hooves as they came to a stop, The Kid saw that the man was totally bald. The thick muscles of his arms and shoulders stretched the faded red fabric of the upper half of a set of long underwear he wore as a shirt. Double bandoliers of ammunition crisscrossed over his barrel-like chest. He held a Winchester in his right hand.

To the leader's left was a smaller man dressed all in gray, from his hat to his boots. His size didn't make him seem any less dangerous. Those rattlers The Kid had killed hadn't been very big, either, but they were deadly nonetheless. In fact, the dark eyes in the man's lean, pockmarked face had a reptilian look about them. The Kid noted how the man's hand never strayed far from the butt of the pistol on his hip.

The other three men were more typical hard cases, the sort of gun-wolves that The Kid had encountered on numerous occasions. He didn't discount their threat, but the trio that edged toward him and the young woman garnered most of his attention. He'd kill the big, bearded man first, if it came to that, he decided, then the little hombre in gray, and then the bald-headed varmint. Once the three of them were dead, he'd use what was left of his life to try for the others. He was pretty sure he'd have some lead in him by that point, though.

White teeth suddenly shone brilliantly in the leader's beard as he grinned. "Been stompin' some snakes, huh?" he asked in a friendly voice.

The Kid wasn't fooled. The man's eyes were just as cold and flinty as they had been before.

"That's right," The Kid said. "Looks like you've got some diamondbacks around here."

The man threw back his head and guffawed. As the echoes from the booming laughter died away, he said, "Hell, yeah, we do. Why do you think they call this Rattlesnake Valley?"

"I didn't know they did," The Kid replied with a shake of his head.

"You're a stranger to these parts, huh?" The man looked at the young woman. "You should've warned your friend what he was gettin' into, Diana."

"He's not my friend," she said. "I never saw him before until a few minutes ago."

"Is that so?" The black-bearded giant sounded like he didn't believe her. His eyes narrowed. "And here I thought your uncle had gone and hired himself a fast gun."

The woman shook her head. "He's a stranger here, Malone. Why don't you let him just turn around and ride away?"

"Why, who's stoppin' him?" The man called Malone grinned at The Kid and went on in an oily tone of mock friendliness, "You just go right ahead and mount up, mister. We wouldn't want to keep you from goin' back to wherever you came from."

The Kid had a feeling that if he got on the buckskin and headed west through the pass, he wouldn't make it twenty yards before he had a bullet in his back. He said, "What if I want to ride on down the valley?"

Malone rubbed the fingers of his left hand over his beard. "Well, I ain't so sure that'd be a good idea. We got all the people we need in the valley right now."

"It's a public road, isn't it?"

"Not exactly. There's supposed to be a marker here so folks will know they're enterin' Trident range, and they'd be better off turnin' around."

"That's not true," Diana said with a sudden flare of anger. "The boundaries of your ranch don't extend this far, Malone. You're claiming range that doesn't belong to you."

He turned a baleful stare on her. "I don't like bein' called a liar, even by a pretty girl like you, Miss Starbird."

The Kid had noticed the brand on the horses

the men rode. It was a line that branched and curved into three points. Now he said, "Neptune's Trident."

That distracted Malone from the young woman named Diana Starbird. He looked at The Kid again and asked, "You know of it?"

"Neptune was the Roman god of the sea, and he was usually depicted carrying a trident like the one you're using as a brand. The Greeks called him Poseidon."

"Didn't expect to run into a man who knows the classics out here in the middle of this godforsaken wilderness," Malone said.

The Kid didn't waste time explaining about his education. He knew that he and Diana were still balanced on the knife-edge of danger from those men.

Yet there was something about Malone, something about the way he looked at Diana, that told he didn't want to hurt the young woman. The Kid's own fate was another story. He had a hunch Malone would kill him without blinking an eye, if the whim struck to do so.

"Is there a town in the valley?"

Malone looked a little surprised by the question. "Aye. Bristol, about fifteen miles east of here."

"I need to replenish my supplies, and my horse could use a little rest before I ride on. I'm not looking for trouble from you or anyone else, Malone. Just let me ride on to the settlement and in a few days I'll be gone."

Malone frowned. "Are you sure Owen Starbird didn't send for you?"

That would be Diana's uncle, The Kid recalled. "Never heard of him until now," he replied honestly.

"Well . . ." Malone scratched at his beard and hesitated as if he were considering what The Kid had said.

While that was going on, the little man in gray turned his horse from the trail and started riding around the area, his eyes directed toward the ground as if he were searching for something. After a moment, he found it. He reined in, dismounted, and reached into the brush to pick up the skull. He turned and held it up to show the others.

"Look at this, Terence."

"My marker," Malone rumbled angrily. "Part of it, anyway."

The bald-headed man pointed toward the trail. "Only one set o' fresh tracks comin' from the west, Terence," he said. "And the bones were there earlier. I seen 'em with my own eyes."

Malone glared at The Kid. "That means you disturbed my marker, mister . . . what is your name, anyway?"

"It's Morgan."

Malone smiled, but his eyes were flintier than ever. "Like Henry Morgan, God rest his soul."

Or like Frank Morgan, The Kid thought. But he didn't mention his father, the notorious gunfighter known as The Drifter. He fought his own battles these days, with no help from anyone.

He recognized the name Henry Morgan, though. He had no doubt that Malone was referring to the infamous English buccaneer from the seventeenth century who had led a fleet of pirate ships against the Spaniards in the Caribbean and Central America and captured Panama City. The skull and crossbones that had been planted in the trail left no doubt about Malone's interest in pirates and piracy.

"I've been known to let travelers use this trail, Mr. Morgan," Malone went on, "if they can pay tribute. I'm afraid I can't do that with you, though."

"Just as well . . . because I don't intend to pay you one red cent."

Malone's lips drew back from his teeth. "Destroyin' my marker is like a slap in the face, Morgan, and I can't allow you to go unpunished for that. You can go on down the trail . . . but you'll have to go past either Greavy"—he nodded to the small, gray-clad gunman—"or Wolfram." A jerk of the bearded chin indicated the bald-headed man. "Guns or fists, Morgan. It's up to you."

Wolfram held up his right hand and opened and closed it into a fist as he grinned at The Kid. He flexed those strong, knobby-knuckled fingers and chuckled.

Greavy's face was cold and expressionless. He was clearly the fast gun of the bunch. The Kid was confident that he could beat Greavy to the draw, but if he did, that didn't mean the others would let him pass. They might just use the shooting as an excuse to kill him.

But if he took on the bruiser called Wolfram and bested him in single combat, that might be different. The rest of them might be impressed enough by such a victory to let him go. More importantly, such an outcome wouldn't expose Diana Starbird to the danger of flying bullets.

And the anger that was always seething not far below the surface of The Kid's mind would have an outlet again.

The Kid looked at Malone and said, "I have your word of honor that if I defeat one of them, you'll allow me to ride on to Bristol?"

"Word of honor," Malone said. He looked at his other men. "You hear that? If Morgan lives, no one bothers him . . . today."

The Kid caught that important distinction but didn't challenge it. First things first. He added, "And Miss Starbird comes with me, either to the settlement or wherever else she wants to go."

Malone frowned. "Diana knows I'd never harm a hair on her head, and none of my men would dare to do so, either. I think the world of her."

"Then you wouldn't want to hold her against her will, would you?"

Before Malone could answer, Diana stepped closer to The Kid and said in a quiet voice, "You don't have to do this on my account, Mr. Morgan. I'll be all right."

"You don't want to stay here, do you?"

She shot a glance at Malone and his men and admitted, "Well . . . no."

"Then you're coming with me." His words had a tone of finality to them.

"It's mighty confident you are that you're goin' to live through this," Malone said. "Greavy is a talented man with a gun, and I've seen Wolfram break bigger fellas than you in half with his bare hands."

"I'll risk it," The Kid said. He took off his hat and handed it to Diana, who had a worried look on her face as she took it. The Kid didn't want to demonstrate his own gun-handling prowess just yet, since it might come in handy later if he needed to take them by surprise, so he unbuckled his gunbelt and handed it to the young woman as well. Then he stripped off his coat and dropped it on the ground. "I'll take on Wolfram."

The bald-headed man had already figured that out. Grinning, he slid the rifle he carried into its saddle boot and swung down from the back of his horse. He didn't wear a handgun, but he had a knife sheathed at his waist. He removed the sheath from his belt and tucked it into a saddlebag, then took off his derby and hung it on the saddle horn.

"I'm gonna enjoy this," he said as he turned toward The Kid, who was rolling up his sleeves while Diana stood there looking more frightened by the second.

"Bust him up good, Wolfram," called one of the other men.

"Yeah," another man added in a raucous shot. "Show him he can't mess with us."

Wolfram started forward, moving at a slow, deliberate pace as he approached The Kid. He was still grinning and flexing his fists. The Kid stood there, arms at his sides, apparently waiting calmly even though his blood surged at the prospect of battle.

Wolfram charged without warning, swinging a malletlike fist at The Kid's head with surprising quickness, and the battle was on.

Chapter 3

The Kid moved with the same sort of speed he exhibited when he drew his gun—fast. He ducked under the looping punch that Wolfram threw and sprang aside from the bull-like charge.

Wolfram's momentum carried him past his intended victim. The Kid kicked out behind him as Wolfram went by, driving the heel of his boot into the back of Wolfram's left knee. The bald-headed bruiser howled in pain and pitched toward the ground as his leg folded up beneath him.

The Kid whirled toward him, intending to kick Wolfram in the head and finish the fight in a hurry, but to his surprise he saw that Wolfram had slapped a hand on the ground and managed to keep from falling. A supple twist of the big body brought Wolfram upright again, facing The Kid. The lips under the handlebar mustache pulled back in an ugly grin.

"Well, now I know you're fast, you little son of

a bitch," Wolfram said as he began to circle more warily toward The Kid. He limped slightly on the leg that had been kicked. "I won't make that mistake again."

The Kid knew his chances of surviving the fight had just decreased since he hadn't been able to dispose of his opponent quickly. But the battle was far from over. True, Wolfram had advantages in height, weight, and reach, but as Conrad Browning, The Kid had been a boxing champion during his college days.

More importantly, his vengeance quest as Kid Morgan and the wandering existence on the frontier that had followed it had taught him to do whatever was necessary to win when he was fighting for his life.

He didn't hang back and let Wolfram bring the fight to him again. Instead he launched an attack of his own, darting in to throw a flurry of punches. The blows were almost too fast for the eye to follow, and they were too fast for Wolfram to block all of them. A couple of The Kid's punches got through, hard shots that landed cleanly on Wolfram's shelflike jaw and rocked his head back and forth.

Wolfram roared in anger and counterattacked, managing to thud a fist into The Kid's breastbone with staggering force. The impact stole his breath away and sent him stumbling backward a few steps.

Wolfram bellowed again—obviously, he was one of those fighters who liked his battles noisy— and surged forward to press his advantage. As The

Kid gasped for air, he saw the light of bloodlust shining in Wolfram's eyes and knew his opponent thought the fight was just about over.

The Kid went low again, sliding under pile driver punches that would have broken his neck if they had landed. He threw his body against Wolfram's knees in a vicious block that cut the man's legs out from under him. Wolfram wasn't able to recover and he went down hard, his face diving into the dirt.

The Kid rolled and came up fast. He'd managed to get a little breath back in his lungs. His heart pounded madly in his chest and his pulse played a trip-hammer symphony inside his skull. He leaped and came down on top of Wolfram, digging both knees into the small of the man's back as hard as he could. Wolfram jerked his head up and yelled in pain.

That gave The Kid the chance to slide his right arm around Wolfram's neck from behind. He grabbed his right wrist with his left hand and hung on for dear life as he tightened the pressure on his opponent's throat. He kept his knees planted in Wolfram's back and hunkered low so that the awkward, frantic blows Wolfram aimed behind him couldn't do any real damage. The Kid forced Wolfram's head back harder and harder and knew that if he kept it up, sooner or later the man's spine would crack.

Wolfram might pass out from lack of air first, though, and he appeared to know it. In desperation, he rolled over and over. The Kid felt the big man's weight crushing him each time he wound up on the bottom, but he didn't let that dislodge his grip. He clung to Wolfram's back like a tick.

Suddenly, he felt Wolfram's muscles go limp. Either the man had lost consciousness, or he was trying to trick The Kid into relaxing that death grip. The Kid wasn't going to be fooled. The muscles of his arms and shoulders bunched. One more good heave would break the bastard's neck—

A shot crashed like thunder. The Kid's head jerked up. He saw that Malone had dismounted and loomed over him, blotting out the sun as he aimed one of those pearl-handled revolvers at The Kid's head. Smoke curled from the barrel as a result of the warning shot Malone had fired.

"Let him go," Malone said. "You're gonna kill him. Let him go, Morgan."

"He would've . . . killed me . . . if he could," The Kid said between clenched teeth.

"I reckon that's right, but I've got the gun, and I'm tellin' you to let him go. We been partners too long for me to let you just snap his neck like that."

"You'll keep your word and let me and Miss Starbird go on to Bristol?"

"Aye, go and be damned!"

The reluctance with which Malone uttered the words convinced The Kid that he was telling the truth. The Kid eased his grip on Wolfram's throat, then released it entirely. The man's head slumped forward into the dirt. He was out cold, all right, not shamming. But he was still alive. The Kid heard the ragged rasp of breath in Wolfram's throat.

With an effort, The Kid kept his muscles from trembling as he climbed to his feet. He didn't want Malone to see how shaky he felt. Instead he reached out to Diana as she came closer to him, took the gun belt from her, and buckled it around his hips. The weight of the holstered Colt felt good to him.

"For your own benefit, you ought to keep movin' instead of stoppin' in Bristol," Malone went on. "There's no place in this valley that'll be safe for you after today."

"Then if I see you or any of your men again, I might as well go ahead and shoot on sight, is that what you're telling me?" The Kid asked.

Malone's lips twisted in a snarl, but he didn't say anything else. He slid his gun back into leather, then bent to grasp one of Wolfram's arms. Without being told to, a couple of the hard cases dismounted and hurried over to help their boss hoist Wolfram's senseless form back on his feet. Wolfram began to come to, shaking his head groggily.

The Kid took his hat from Diana and put it on, then picked up his coat, folded it, and stuck it in his saddlebags. The sun was too hot for the garment.

He asked in a low voice, "Where's your horse?"

She inclined her head toward the boulders where she had been hidden as she watched him kick the skull out of the trail. He figured he hadn't heard her ride up because the echoes of his shot had been rolling away over the hills at the time.

"Go get it," he told her.

"Not yet," she replied. "Not until they're gone."

He understood what she meant. She believed that Malone would be less likely to break his word and try to gun The Kid down as long as she was close by.

She was probably right about that. He stood there holding the buckskin's reins in his left hand and kept his right close to his gun. Greavy kept a close eye on The Kid while Malone and his men helped Wolfram climb onto his horse. The Kid had a feeling that Greavy sensed the presence of another fast gun. He saw the appraisal and the challenge in the little man's eyes. Greavy was trying to figure out if he could take The Kid.

Once Wolfram was mounted again, Malone swung up onto his own saddle and motioned for his men to follow suit. They turned their horses around and started jogging away, following the trail that led through the valley. They rounded a bend and rode out of sight.

"Do you think they'll try to find a place to pull an ambush?" The Kid asked.

Diana shook her head. "Not now. Black Terence keeps his word . . . most of the time."

The Kid glanced over at her and lifted an eyebrow.

Diana waved a hand and said, "I'll explain on the way to Diamondback."

"Diamondback?"

"The ranch my uncle and I own."

"I was headed for Bristol, remember?"

Diana shook her head. "Not anymore. It won't be safe for you. I'm pretty sure Malone has spies working for him in town. Anyway, there are a lot of alleys where bushwhackers could hide."

"You don't owe me anything, if that's what you're thinking," The Kid told her.

Diana let out a snort. "Me owe you anything? It's the other way around, Mr. Morgan. If I hadn't been here, Malone and his men would have killed you. It was your shot that drew them in the first place. When you saw the skull and crossbones, why didn't you just turn around and ride away? Don't you know what they mean?" She drew in a deep breath. "They mean death."

The Kid wasn't in any mood to argue with her. "I've seen plenty of it," he said. "Let's get your horse."

"You'll come to the ranch with me?"

The Kid shrugged. "Why not? The main thing I wanted was a chance to rest my buckskin. I reckon I can do that at your place as well as I can in town."

"Better," Diana said. "Our hands will take good care of your horse."

They fetched her mount, a fine-looking chestnut, from the rocks where she had left it. She put her foot in the stirrup and stepped up in to the saddle with a lithe grace that didn't surprise The Kid. From everything he had seen so far, he guessed that she had been born and raised in West Texas. He knew a Western girl when he saw one. He had married one, in fact, and a pang went through him at the reminder of what he had lost. Months had passed since Rebel's death, but he still reacted the same way every time he thought about her.

As they started along the trail, he kept his eyes peeled for any sign of trouble, just in case Diana was wrong about Malone and his men trying to ambush them. The range seemed peaceful enough, though.

"Where is this Diamondback ranch?" The Kid asked.

Diana pointed to the line of trees that marked the stream's course. "Everything in the valley north of the Severn River is Diamondback range."

"The Severn, eh?" That was the name of a river in England, he recalled, and Bristol, of course, was an English town. He wondered if that meant anything. He had been to England, and while Rattlesnake Valley certainly wasn't as dry and barren as most of West Texas, it was still a far cry from the lush green English countryside.

Diana didn't offer any explanations. She was watchful, too, as if she didn't have complete confidence in her assurances that Malone wouldn't attack them.

"Why the skull and crossbones?" The Kid asked after they had ridden a mile or so. "I know they put it on the labels of liquids that are poisonous, but I never saw anybody use it as a road marker before."

"It's the symbol from the pirate flag," Diana said, telling The Kid something he already knew. "I suppose Malone thinks that it's appropriate."

"Appropriate?" The Kid repeated. He frowned over at her. "Are you telling me that—"

"Black Terence Malone is a pirate," Diana said with a nod. "At least, he used to be, and just because he's not on the high seas anymore, doesn't mean he's any less of a brigand."

Chapter 4

The Kid looked at her in silence for a long moment, then said, "You're going to have to explain that. I suppose it has something to do with Malone being known as Black Terence."

She nodded. "That's right. Twenty years ago, Malone was a pirate in the Caribbean Sea. He'd been a sailor on a blockade runner for the Confederacy during the War of Northern Aggression, and after the war was over, he took what he'd learned and put it to use for himself. He got a ship, gathered a crew of like-minded men, and started raiding the shipping lanes. He looted and sunk a number of British cargo vessels. The Royal Navy sent warships after him, but Malone had learned how to dodge pursuit so effectively that he was able to avoid capture for several years."

"But they finally got him?" The Kid guessed.

"That's right." Diana smiled. "HMS *Scorpion*, commanded by Captain Owen Starbird, sunk

Malone's ship and fished him and the other survivors from his crew out of the water."

"Your uncle?"

She shook her head. "That's right."

"The one who owns this Diamondback Ranch where you're taking me?"

"Actually, he only owns half of it. The other half is mine, but Uncle Owen has been running things ever since my father died and left the spread to us."

The Kid's keen eyes habitually checked their surroundings again but didn't see any sign of danger. Some birds flew overhead, but their pace was lazy. Nothing had spooked them.

"Keep talking," he told Diana.

"Why? You don't actually deserve an explanation, you know. It's not like I owe you anything."

"Just call it curiosity," The Kid said.

"Downright nosiness, if you ask me."

The Kid smiled instead of getting offended at her comment. "I've been known to poke my nose where it doesn't necessarily belong," he admitted.

"Well, don't think that you're going to get in the middle of this fracas. If you're smart, you'll mind your own business and get on out of Rattlesnake Valley as fast as you can."

"Then tell me what I'll be running away from."

Diana sighed. "All right. My father was George Starbird. He was his father's third son. Uncle Owen was the second. Do you know what that means?"

"The law of primogeniture," The Kid replied without hesitation. "Neither of them could inherit the family title and estate because they weren't the firstborn son."

Diana's eyes narrowed in surprise. Obviously, she hadn't expected such a well-informed answer from him. "How do you know that?" she asked.

"I've done some reading in my time," The Kid answered vaguely, keeping his true background to himself as always. "I suppose that's why your uncle went into the Royal Navy and your father immigrated to America. British nobility tends not to want those second and third sons hanging around and maybe doing something to embarrass the family."

"That's exactly right. The two of them had to get out and make lives for themselves. My father could have gone into the military or the diplomatic service, but he decided that he wanted the adventure of coming to the United States. His family gave him enough money to get here."

"So he was a remittance man," The Kid said.

Diana shook her head again. "No, they didn't keep paying him to stay out of sight and out of mind. They paid for his passage over here, and that was it. He wanted to come west, so he worked at odd jobs and finally saved enough to take a train from New York to Pittsburgh. From there he got a job on a steamship that carried freight up and down the Ohio River. That eventually got him to the Mississippi and a similar job there, and then he joined a wagon train heading for Santa Fe. He did a little bit of everything—fur trapping, packing for the army, prospecting, things like that—and during the war he left New Mexico Territory and came here to West Texas. It was a pretty wild place then."

The Kid nodded. "I've heard stories," he said, without mentioning who he'd heard them from.

"He had saved enough money to buy a small, failed ranch, here in what was already called Rattlesnake Valley. It was a different place then. The stream was dry most of the year, and even when there was water in it, there wasn't enough to grow grass to support a herd of cattle. But my father had the idea that if there was a little water, there might be more at the source. He'd had some classes in the natural sciences before he left England and thought the streambed looked like it had once been larger. He traced the stream up into the mountains and found the springs that fed it. Sure enough, sometime in the past a rockslide had partially blocked the springs, so that only a small trickle of water was getting out through the rocks. He worked for months, by himself, clearing the slide, and finally the river was flowing again the way it once had. That was when the valley began to green up and started becoming the fine place to live and raise cattle that it is today."

Diana reached for the canteen hung on her saddle. While she was drinking, The Kid thought about what she had said and then asked, "How did he wind up owning all the range in the valley north of the river?"

Diana smiled as she put the cap back on the canteen. "My father was a canny man, Mr. Morgan, and a stubborn one. He had a dream, and he came to believe that Rattlesnake Valley was where it would be fulfilled. With every penny he could scrape up, he bought more land *before* he got the river flowing again. It was a gamble, but he borrowed money, worked for other men, did anything and everything he could to acquire more range, because he believed it would be valuable someday. Then, suddenly, he was right. He became a rich man almost overnight when the wilderness began to bloom."

The Kid nodded. Some people would look at a man like George Starbird and think that he must have been lucky, that he didn't really deserve the success he'd had. They would be jealous because they didn't see—or chose not to see—the years of hard work and preparation that Starbird had put in before fortune ever smiled on him.

"There was no settlement in the valley then," Diana went on, "so he founded Bristol, naming it after a city near the place he had grown up in England."

"I reckon that's how the river got its name, too."

She nodded. "That's right. My father loved this country and was glad he came here, but he still had a lot of fondness for his homeland."

"Can't blame a man for that," The Kid said.

"Starting up the town made Father even wealthier.

He was still a young man, though, and he realized he was missing something."

"A wife," The Kid guessed.

"Exactly. One of the men who came to Bristol to start a store when it was nothing more than a cluster of tents and shacks had a daughter, and when my father met her, he knew she was the one he wanted." Diana laughed softly. "Luckily for me, she felt the same way about him. They were married less than six months later, and in time, I came along."

"No brothers or sisters?" The Kid asked, then realized that maybe he was prying.

Diana's expression grew solemn. "No. A fever took her when I was less than two years old."

"I'm sorry."

"I never knew her," she went on. "All I've seen are pictures of her . . . and the way my father's eyes were always haunted by her loss." Diana paused and looked off to the side of the trail, obviously struggling with her feelings for a moment before resuming. "But my father had a ranch to run and a daughter to raise, so he set about doing both of those things to the best of his ability."

"I had a feeling you were born and raised out here, from the way you ride and handle a rifle."

She laughed. "I was riding before I could walk, and shooting not long after that. My father didn't raise me to be the son he never had, or anything like that, but he wanted to be sure I could take care of myself." She paused again. "I can."

The Kid didn't doubt it.

He said, "I'm surprised he didn't wind up owning the entire valley. Seems like it would have been easy enough for him to do."

"It would have," Diana agreed, "but he didn't want to. He said he had plenty of range for his own needs, and that if somebody else wanted to work hard and make something for themselves, they ought to have the chance. He didn't try to stop anyone from coming into the valley and starting up small spreads south of the river, and he never hogged the water or anything like that. He was a good man, Mr. Morgan. If you want to boil everything down to its basics, that's it right there. He was a good man."

"He sounds like it," The Kid agreed. "But he wasn't immortal, was he?"

With a sad smile on her face, she shook her head. "No," she said. "He wasn't immortal."

"What happened?"

She looked over at him and said, "You really are curious, aren't you?"

"I mean no offense," The Kid told her. "But you started this story, and I'd like to hear the end of it."

"I suppose I can't blame you for that." She looked off again. "It's only been a couple of years, and it still hurts." She drew in a breath. "My father knew how to handle horses as well as anybody I ever saw. But that didn't help him one day when one of those damned snakes slithered right under the hooves of the horse he was riding, right outside the barn. It took them both by surprise. The horse went up in the air, my father came out of the saddle . . . He broke his neck when he landed. He lived for about eight hours before passing away that night."

The Kid let the silence stretch out for a moment before he said, "That's a rough thing."

"It could have been worse. At least I got a chance to say good-bye to him. And he had a chance to tell me that he'd already sent for Uncle Owen to come and settle on Diamondback after he retired from the Royal Navy. It was supposed to be a surprise for me. Well, it was, all right."

Something about her tone of voice told The Kid that it hadn't necessarily been a good surprise. He wondered how Diana and her uncle got along and if she resented him for inheriting half the ranch where she had grown up. She might feel that everything should have gone to her, but that had been George Starbird's decision to make.

"How does this tie in with Malone? He went to prison for being a pirate, I reckon."

"Of course he did. But he didn't go to the gallows, because he and his men always spared the crews of the ships they captured. He was behind bars for eighteen years." Diana laughed again, but the sound had an edge to it. "He was released not long after Uncle Owen retired from the Royal Navy."

"And he came here to settle the score for all

those years he was locked up," The Kid said as understanding dawned in him.

Diana looked over at him. "That's right, Mr. Morgan. Black Terence Malone came here to hoist the Jolly Roger over West Texas and destroy Owen Starbird."

Chapter 5

The Kid looked at her and tried not to laugh at that Jolly Roger comment. It was obvious that she was dead serious in what she had just said. Thinking back over what had happened, he supposed she had a right to be. His chest still ached where Wolfram had landed that punch.

"So Malone tracked your uncle to this valley, then came here and bought a ranch."

"The Bar SW, old Silas Wilmott's place. Silas passed away about a year and a half ago. A few months after that, Malone showed up with title to the place. He had bought it from Silas's heirs, who live up in Dallas."

"If he was legally released from prison in England, there's nothing stopping him from doing something like that."

"I know. Uncle Owen told me not to worry about it. He said that Malone was just trying to make him nervous. But he brought some of his old crew of cutthroats with him, men like Wolfram and Greavy, and he hired more men whose hands didn't get calluses from using a rope, if you know what I mean."

The Kid knew very well what she meant. He had seen the gunmen with Malone with his own eyes. A rancher hired men like that for only one reason—to fight.

"Does he have any actual punchers?"

Diana shrugged. "A few. Enough to handle the small herd that was left on the Bar SW. Of course, since Malone changed the brand to the Trident, his herd has grown some."

"Rustling?" The Kid guessed.

"That's what Uncle Owen and I believe. Our herds have shrunk steadily while Malone's has been growing. You can draw your own conclusions."

"Has the law tried to do anything about it?"

"Malone's too slick. Nobody has been able to catch him breaking the law. Anyway, there's just a single deputy sheriff in Bristol, sent down from the county seat to handle the whole valley. He can't be everywhere at once."

"Has anything else odd been going on?"

"Would you call having several Diamondback hands being bushwhacked odd?" Diana's mouth tightened into a grim line. "Two of them are dead, and the others were wounded. The shootings always happened when one of our men was out on the range alone. The hands have stopped riding by themselves. They always go out in groups now, but that means we're spread pretty thin. It hasn't helped that some of our men have quit. You can't blame them for leaving this part of the country, though. No one wants to get shot down from an ambush."

As she described it, it was a bad situation, all right. The Kid had heard Frank Morgan talk about similar setups. Even the biggest rancher could be brought low by rustlers chipping away at his herds and demoralizing his crew into quitting. From the sound of it, Owen Starbird had plenty of trouble on his plate.

Starbird's trouble was none of his business, though, The Kid told himself. He had felt an instinctive dislike for Malone, Greavy, and Wolfram, but that was no reason for him to hang around Rattlesnake Valley and involve himself in the dangerous conflicts going on there.

He and Diana had reached a trail that veered off to the north from the main road. Diana turned her chestnut onto it, and The Kid rode alongside her on the buckskin. He had a hunch this trail led to the headquarters of Diamondback.

A few minutes later, they came to the river. The stream spread out about sixty feet wide between grassy banks, and it was shallow enough that The Kid could see the gravel bed. The water jumped and bubbled around some rocks that jutted up fifty yards downstream. The Severn was a nice little river, and since it was spring fed, it had a good steady flow. The Kid and Diana forded it with ease, then continued northward.

"How does Malone get away with trying to block off the trail into the valley?" The Kid asked.

"In the time he's been here, he's bought some other small spreads and expanded his ranch. The trail cuts through part of his range, and he takes that to mean that he controls the entire length of it."

"There's no legal basis for that. Folks out here always have a right of free passage."

"Traditionally, maybe. I suppose if he wanted to, he could fence off just the part of the trail that's on his land and charge a toll to use it. That's what Uncle Owen thinks, anyway. But Malone's not really interested in doing that. He just wants to intimidate everyone in the valley and make sure that they're too scared to stand up to him while he goes after Diamondback. There were a couple of small ranchers who spoke out against Malone, and they wound up with their barns being burned down in the middle of the night and their houses shot up. It's just pure luck no one has been killed except for a couple of our men."

"Sounds to me like Malone's just running roughshod over folks around here."

"That's what he's doing, Mr. Morgan. That's exactly what he's doing. And so far, Uncle Owen and I are really the only ones who are trying to fight him."

The Kid looked around. They were passing through gently rolling hills dotted with stands of trees and an occasional rocky outcropping. It was good range, he thought, and well worth fighting for. He could understand why Diana and her uncle would stand up to Malone and his reign of terror. They needed help, though, from the other people in the valley, and evidently they weren't getting it.

"What were you doing riding alone up there around the pass?" he asked her.

She bristled at the question. "I told you, I can take care of myself. I don't let Malone dictate where I can ride."

"Yeah, I sort of felt the same way when I saw that skull and crossbones in the trail," The Kid drawled.

Diana glared at him for a second, then shrugged. "I'd ridden up there to check on an old Indian who lives in the mountains. He befriended my father years ago when my father first came to the valley. That was another thing my father asked me to do while he was dying—to look after his old friend."

"That's an admirable thing to do," The Kid said. "Maybe you should take some guards with you next time, though."

Diana shook her head. "That's not necessary. Malone won't hurt me."

"How do you know that? Seems to me like hurting you would be a good way for him to get back at your uncle."

"No, he has something even more diabolical than that in mind. He wants to *marry* me."

The Kid grunted. "Yeah, marrying somebody, that's pretty diabolical, all right."

Diana surprised him again by blushing. He

watched the pink flush spread prettily over her face as she said, "When Malone first showed up, he rode over to our ranch by himself. He said he'd heard about me in town and decided to come courting. He announced then and there that he intended to marry me and combine Diamondback and Trident." She sighed. "I wish Uncle Owen had gone ahead and shot him, right then and there. Ever since then, every time Malone catches me alone, he . . . he tries to . . . seduce me."

She was lucky he hadn't done worse than that, The Kid thought. A man like Malone was used to taking what he wanted, whether it was money or power or land . . . or a woman.

"That's another good reason you shouldn't ride out alone," The Kid told her.

"You're not my father or my uncle, Mr. Morgan," she shot back. "In fact, a couple of hours ago I had never even laid eyes on you. So I don't much like the idea of you telling me what to do."

The Kid shook his head. "Just offering an opinion, that's all. You're free to take it for what it's worth, or not."

They rode along in tense silence for a few more minutes, then topped a rise and looked at a big, whitewashed, two-story house surrounded by cottonwoods and flanked by barns, corrals, a bunkhouse, and other outbuildings.

"That's it," Diana said with a nod. "Diamond-back."

"Looks like a fine spread," The Kid said.

"It is. The finest in this part of Texas. That's why Uncle Owen and I are damned if we'll let Black Terence Malone buffalo us!"

The vehemence in Diana's voice made The Kid smile. He had liked her on sight, and although she could be a mite testy, he liked her even more since he had gotten to know her a little.

That didn't mean he was going to involve himself in her troubles, though. He had spent months in grief and sorrow, along with the rage and thirst for vengeance that had driven him to find his wife's killers and bring them to justice—his own brand of justice. Once he had accomplished that, most of the anger had bled away from his soul, but the sadness was still there. He supposed it always would be, even though he sometimes told himself it was time to move on with his life. Convincing himself of that hadn't proven to be easy.

Probably because he didn't really want to move on. He just wanted to be alone with his grief. But instead he seemed to keep running in to folks who could use a helping hand—especially if that hand was fast on the draw and accurate with a gun. He had been drawn by chance into several dangerous situations that had come damn close to getting him killed, and he was tired of it.

Diana and her uncle could handle Malone, he thought. They had this big ranch and a crew that was probably pretty tough. Frontiersmen fought their own battles. Stomped their own snakes.

That thought made a smile pull at his mouth.

Even though he had crushed that second rattler's skull, if Diana hadn't plugged it first with her rifle, the scaly creature might have gotten him. He supposed he owed her a little something for that. She had offered him the hospitality of her home, too, declaring that he would be safer there than in Bristol. Considering all that, he wasn't sure he could ride away and leave her to the mercy of Terence Malone.

A couple of big yellow dogs ran out to meet them as they rode up to the ranch headquarters. The loud barking brought men from the barn. The Kid noticed immediately that they were all armed with handguns, and two of them carried Winchesters. A display of that much armament so close to home meant there was trouble in those parts, all right.

A stocky man with a bushy gray mustache came over to them as they reined their horses to a halt in front of the house. Diana smiled at him and said, "Hello, Sam."

"Miss Diana," the man replied as he touched the brim of his old battered black hat. He nodded toward The Kid and added, "Who's the stray?"

"This is Mr. Morgan," she said. "Mr. Morgan, Sam Rocklin, our foreman."

"Pleased to meet you, mister," Rocklin said, but a definite look of suspicion remained in his eyes. "Where'd you run into Miss Diana?"

"Out on the western trail just below the pass," Diana replied before The Kid could say anything. "Malone put a skull and crossbones in the trail."

"What!" Rocklin's face darkened with anger. "Why, that mangy—"

Thumping sounds from the house cut his exclamation short. The Kid, Diana, and Sam Rocklin all turned their heads to look in that direction.

The screen door swung open, and a man levered his bulky body out onto the porch using a pair of crutches that supported his heavy torso where his wasted legs could not.

Chapter 6

The man had iron-gray hair and a precisely clipped mustache. His weathered, ruddy face spoke of a life lived outdoors—in Owen Starbird's case, on the sea. He wore boots, jeans, and a cowhide vest over a butternut shirt, but his bearing made the range clothes look like a uniform.

"You didn't tell me you were leaving, Diana," he said in a British accent as a frown creased his forehead. "I'd appreciate being kept informed of such things. I was quite concerned about your well-being."

"I would think you'd know by now, Uncle Owen, that I come and go as I please," Diana replied. Her soft Texas drawl was in sharp contrast to his clipped tones, and it seemed odd that they were uncle and niece, yet shared so little in common. Of course, they came from completely different backgrounds, The Kid reminded himself. They were linked by blood, but nothing else.

Starbird switched his eagle-eyed gaze to The Kid. "Who's this?" he demanded.

"Mr. Morgan. I'm afraid I don't know his first name."

"Just call me Kid."

Starbird snorted. "Kid Morgan. That sounds like a name from one of your lurid American dime novels."

He was closer to right about that than he knew. The Kid had been inspired by those very dime novels—some of them about his own father—when he made up the name.

Trying to be civil, he said, "I'm pleased to meet you, Mr. Starbird."

"Captain Starbird," the Englishman corrected him. "Even though I'm retired, I'm still entitled to use my rank."

The Kid nodded. "Fine. Pleased to meet you, Captain."

"Hmmph," Starbird said. "Diana, what's going on here? Who is this man? Where have you been?"

"That's a lot of questions, and the sun's hot," Diana said. She swung down from the saddle. "Let's go inside where it's cooler. Please come in, Mr. Morgan."

"I appreciate the hospitality," The Kid said with a slight smile as he dismounted.

"Sam, would you see to Mr. Morgan's horse?" Diana asked.

The stocky foreman nodded and reached for the

buckskin's reins. "Sure thing, Miss Diana. We'll take good care of your hoss, mister."

The Kid handed over the reins. Diana gave Rocklin the reins to her chestnut as well, and he led both mounts toward the barn.

The Kid waved a hand toward the steps leading up to the porch. "After you, Miss Starbird." She smiled and nodded.

Her uncle still looked angry and upset. "I don't recall inviting you in, sir," he snapped.

"This is as much my house as it is yours, Uncle Owen," Diana said, "and I intend to be hospitable to Mr. Morgan. We had a run-in with Malone and some of his men."

"Malone!" Starbird burst out. "My God! Are you all right? Did that bloody—I mean, that blasted pirate—hurt you?"

"I'm fine," Diana assured him. She and The Kid reached the welcome shade of the porch. "Mr. Morgan had a tussle with Wolfram, though."

Starbird's head jerked toward The Kid. "And you're still alive?" He sounded like he couldn't believe it.

"Apparently," The Kid said.

"Wolfram is a monster," Starbird said. "In the old days, he was the most feared of Malone's crew of cutthroats . . . after Black Terence himself, of course. No offense, Morgan, but I find it difficult to accept the idea that a man such as yourself bested him."

"You can believe it," Diana said. "I saw it with

my own eyes. Malone gave Mr. Morgan the choice of going up against Wolfram or drawing against Greavy."

Starbird made a face like there was a bad taste in his mouth. "Greavy," he repeated. "That one's a bad lot, too." With a sigh, he turned, his crutches clumping on the porch planks. "Well, come inside. As Diana said, we might as well be where it's cooler."

The Kid followed them into the house and found himself in a big, well-appointed room. Indian rugs covered the floor. The sofas and chairs were made of thick wooden beams and upholstered with leather-covered cushions. A massive fireplace filled half of one wall, and above the mantel the heads of elk, antelope, and mountain goats were mounted, along with a tawny mountain lion with its teeth bared in the midst of a snarl. The Kid figured George Starbird had bagged those trophies, although having seen Diana handle a rifle, it wouldn't have surprised him if she turned out to be responsible for a few of them.

A heavyset Mexican woman came in to the room through a door that led to the rest of the house. Starbird told her, "Bring us some cool lemonade, Carmelita."

The woman nodded. "*Sí, Capitán.*"

Even the servants used Starbird's rank, The Kid noted.

Starbird made his way over to a wheelchair, turned, and lowered himself into it. He set his crutches aside, then picked up each leg in turn and placed his feet on the footrests attached to the chair. The scowl on Starbird's face told The Kid that the man hated being crippled. Clearly, since he had captained a ship in the Royal Navy, Starbird hadn't always been lacking the use of his legs. The Kid wondered what had happened, but he figured if anybody wanted to tell him, they would.

The sight of Starbird sitting in the chair made The Kid think of Vernon Moss, one of the outlaws responsible for his wife's death. Moss had been in a wheelchair, too, when The Kid finally caught up to him, but that hadn't stopped the man from trying to shoot it out. It hadn't stopped The Kid from killing him, either. A bullet from a man in a wheelchair could kill you just as dead as if he'd been standing on his own two feet.

The Kid pushed those thoughts away as Starbird placed his hands on his knees, frowned at Diana, and said, "Now, tell me what happened."

She sat down in one of the heavy chairs and gestured for The Kid to take a seat on a sofa that was positioned at a right angle to the chair. "I rode over to the mountains to check on Gray Hawk and make sure he was all right," she began.

"That impudent old Yaqui?" Starbird gave an imperious snort. "Of course he's all right. He's like an ancient lizard. Nothing bothers him."

"Still, I promised Father I'd look in on him from time to time. You know that, Uncle Owen."

"Go on," Starbird said impatiently. "Get to the part about Malone."

"I'm getting there. I was on my way back from Gray Hawk's place when I heard a shot somewhere close by. I thought it might be some of Malone's men trying to ambush me, so I hid in some rocks near the trail. But then I saw Mr. Morgan and realized that he had fired the shot."

Starbird glared at The Kid. "You tried to ambush my niece, sir?"

"Nothing of the sort," Diana said before The Kid could reply. "He'd just shot a snake. Very skillfully, too. He blew its head right off."

"Well . . . I'm glad to hear that," Starbird admitted in a grudging tone. "There are too blasted many of those serpents in this valley."

"It sounds like you need a visit from Saint Patrick," The Kid commented.

"You're familiar with the legend of how he charmed all the snakes out of Ireland?"

Diana said, "Mr. Morgan seems to be surprisingly well-read, Uncle Owen."

Starbird didn't look impressed. He said, "Get on with the story."

"I saw that someone had put a skull and crossbones in the trail, almost certainly as a warning for strangers to keep out of the valley," Diana continued.

Starbird clenched a fist and growled, "That sounds like Malone's work."

Diana nodded. "I thought the same thing. Then

Mr. Morgan kicked the skull out of the trail and threw the other bones into the brush."

Starbird looked at The Kid. "You did that?"

"I didn't like the looks of those bones," he said with a shrug. "It seemed awfully presumptuous to me."

Starbird's gaze rested squarely on The Kid for a moment, and then for the first time, a bit of humor flashed in the former naval officer's stern eyes. "I never cared much for the bloody symbol myself," he said, then glanced at his niece. "Begging your pardon, Diana."

"That's all right, Uncle Owen. I heard worse cussing from the ranch hands by the time I was five."

"I daresay you did. What happened after Mr. Morgan disposed of the skull and crossbones?"

"I had to shoot another rattler that had crawled up without him noticing it."

"So my niece saved your life, Morgan?"

In a manner of speaking, The Kid thought, but he contented himself with saying simply, "That's right."

"The shots drew Malone's attention, though," Diana said. "He came galloping up with Wolfram, Greavy, and three of those hard cases who ride for him. I talked him into letting Mr. Morgan turn around and ride back out of the valley."

Starbird looked at The Kid again. "I see you didn't take that opportunity."

"I ride where I please," The Kid said.

"So you clashed with Wolfram and lived to tell the tale. Very impressive, young man. Who taught you how to fight?"

"Not who. What."

Starbird frowned. "I beg your pardon?"

"It wasn't a person who taught me how to fight," The Kid explained. "It was the whole world."

"Ah." Starbird nodded slowly. "Experience, huh? School of hard knocks and all that?"

"That's right." Morgan didn't see any point in going into detail about just how hard some of those knocks had been.

Diana said, "Malone gave his word that if Mr. Morgan won, no one would bother him, but only for today. Mr. Morgan was planning to ride on to Bristol, but I convinced him to come here to Diamondback instead."

"A wise choice, sir," Starbird said with a nod. "I fear that Bristol isn't the same town it was when my brother founded it. Too many undesirable elements have moved in. The area has a growing reputation for lawlessness, primarily because Malone has gotten away with murder and rustling. Our lone deputy in the valley is overmatched."

"Have you sent word to the Rangers?" The Kid asked.

"A letter has gone to Austin, yes, but there's been no response. I suspect that the Rangers are stretched thin, too, as are all the other forces of law and order on the frontier. Just like Her Majesty's forces were when we were trying to combat the tide of piracy in the Caribbean."

"But you defeated Malone there," The Kid pointed out. "You captured him and sent him to prison."

Starbird looked down at his wasted legs with bitterness in his eyes. "I was a much different man then," he said quietly. "Those days seem to belong to a completely different life."

"My uncle and I just need a little help," Diana said. "Somebody who's a match for Malone and his men." Now that she had started, she didn't hesitate to press on, The Kid noted. "How about it, Mr. Morgan? How would you like a job riding for Diamondback?"

"I'm not a cowhand," The Kid said.

"I'm not talking about that, and you know it," Diana snapped. "I'm talking about gun work. There's going to be plenty of it in Rattlesnake Valley."

Chapter 7

That was putting it plainly enough. The Kid said, "At first Malone seemed to think that I was a hired gun. Is that what *you* think, too, Miss Starbird?"

"Well?" she challenged. "Aren't you?"

"No. I'm not."

She shook her head. "I don't believe you. I saw the way you blasted that rattler's head off with one shot, and I watched while you nearly broke Wolfram's neck. You're a professional fighting man, Mr. Morgan."

She would never believe him if he told her that until a few years earlier, the only real fighting he'd done had been in offices and boardrooms, that his weapons had been money and influence and that when he won a battle, it was usually with the stroke of a pen. She wouldn't believe him, and after everything that had happened to him, he could barely accept the truth of that himself.

"I'm sorry," he said, "but you've got me wrong. I'm not looking for work. Especially not gun work."

"If you think that Malone will pay you more—"

"I wouldn't work for Malone if he had all the pirate treasure of Blackbeard and Captain Kidd put together."

That brought a brusque bark of laughter from Owen Starbird. "I believe you've misjudged our visitor, Diana," he said. "And perhaps insulted him a bit, too."

The Kid lifted a hand to wave that off. "I'm not insulted," he assured them. "But this isn't my war."

"Of course not," Starbird said. "Well, then, if we can't recruit you . . . what can we do for you?"

"My horse needs some rest."

Starbird nodded. "He'll have it, along with plenty of grain and water, for as long as you like."

"And I'm running low on supplies. I planned on picking up some in the next settlement I came to."

"We can spare enough to get you out of the valley and across the desert east of here. There's no need for you to stop in Bristol."

"What's on the other side of that desert?"

"Some more hills, and beyond them the railroad that runs from San Antonio to El Paso. There's a flag stop where you can board the train. We drive our cattle there when it's time to ship them to market. The desert's not as bad as it looks. There's water there, if you know where to find it, and a man on horseback can cross it in a day."

The Kid nodded. "Sounds like my only real problem will be making it to the other end of the valley without Malone catching me. He only ordered his men to leave me alone for the rest of today."

"You should have negotiated a longer truce," Starbird said dryly. "He likely would have gone along with it, believing that he'd never have to honor his word because either Wolfram or Greavy would kill you, whichever of them you chose to face in battle."

The Kid chuckled. "Yeah, I didn't think of it at the time."

The Mexican woman, Carmelita, came in with a pitcher of lemonade and three glasses. She poured the cool, refreshing drinks and served them.

Starbird sipped from his glass and then said, "You're welcome to stay as long as you like, Morgan. I admit, I was a bit suspicious of you at first, but now that I've heard the story, I appreciate you seeing to it that my niece was able to return home safely from her foolish foray."

"Wait a minute," Diana said. "*He* didn't save *me*. Malone wouldn't have hurt me or allowed his men to bother me. You know that, Uncle Owen. If anything, I saved Mr. Morgan's hide by being there. Malone was putting on a show for me by offering that bargain to The Kid."

"Yes, well, you shouldn't have been there in the first place."

Diana sighed in exasperation and shook her head. She took a long swig of the lemonade, then placed her glass on a low table in front of her chair as she stood up.

"I'm going to my room," she said in a chilly voice.

The Kid and Starbird didn't say anything as Diana left the room. When she was gone, Starbird said, "I'm afraid my brother raised his daughter with a rather free hand. She's headstrong, impulsive, lacking in self-discipline, and accustomed to getting her own way. I apologize for any offense she may have given you, Morgan."

"None taken," The Kid said. "I'm sure she's not much like the English ladies you've known, Captain, but an English lady might not survive very long out here."

"You've been to England?"

"I have. My mother and I did the European tour a number of years ago."

"My God. You're not a saddle tramp, are you?"

The Kid smiled. "I wouldn't go so far as to say that. I've been doing a lot of drifting recently."

"Well . . . how would a Texan put it? I hope you'll . . . light and set for a spell, while you're visiting Diamondback."

"Thank you, Captain," The Kid said as his smile widened into a grin. "I believe I will, and I'm much obliged for the hospitality."

* * *

Starbird said that he would have Rocklin bring in The Kid's rifles and saddlebags from the barn, then called Carmelita and ordered her to show The Kid to one of the empty bedrooms on the second floor. Powerful arms straining, Starbird wheeled himself out of the living room as The Kid followed the servant up the stairs.

The room Carmelita took him to was large, airy, and comfortable, with a pair of open windows covered by gauzy curtains that moved back and forth in the hot breeze. A four-poster bed, a couple of chairs, a washstand, and a wardrobe completed the furnishings. The windows afforded a view to the west of the house, toward the mountains.

The Kid nodded in satisfaction, then said, "Thank you, Carmelita." As she started to leave, he gave in to curiosity and stopped her. "I have a question."

"Sí, señor?"

"How long has Captain Starbird been like he is? His legs, I mean."

Carmelita shook her head. *"No habla, señor."*

That was an outright lie, and The Kid knew it. Downstairs, Starbird had given Carmelita her orders in English, and she had seemed to understand them perfectly. But her loyalty to her employer meant that she didn't want to talk about the captain, he supposed, so he didn't press the question. He just smiled, nodded, said, "*Gracias*," and waved her out of the room.

His muscles were starting to ache from the battle with Wolfram, even though he hadn't absorbed as much punishment as he might have expected to in a brawl like that. He'd been riding for days, too, and was tired. He took off his gunbelt, coiled it and placed it on one of the chairs next to the bed. Then he pulled off his boots and shirt and stood next to the washstand as he dipped the cloth in the basin of cool water. It felt good to wipe the dust off his face and torso.

A soft knock sounded on the door. He stepped swiftly to the chair and bent slightly to slide the Colt from its holster. Instinct prompted that move. He didn't have to think about it. Gun in hand, he went to the door and called, "Who is it?"

"Diana Starbird," came the answer from the other side of the panel.

The Kid opened the door. Diana's eyes widened slightly, but whether it was from the sight of his bare chest or the gun in his hand—or both—he didn't know. He smiled and said, "What can I do for you, Miss Starbird?"

"I-I just wanted to see that you had gotten settled in properly and that the room is comfortable."

He nodded. "Very much so. Although I haven't tried out the bed yet. I was just about to do that."

"Well . . . well . . ." Anger suddenly bloomed on her face. "Don't expect me to join you!"

"The thought never entered my mind," The Kid replied coolly.

"I'll just bet!" She turned on her heel and stalked off down the hall.

The Kid laughed and eased the door closed. What he had said to Diana wasn't strictly, completely true. She was a very attractive woman, and he had the same appetites as any normal man, even though he didn't intend to indulge them anytime soon. He wasn't sure you could put a time limit on a period of mourning, say that a certain number of months or years was proper and another wasn't. He was sure that the girl called Elena had expected him to bed her while they were traveling together, but that had never happened. Come to think of it, maybe that was one reason she had left him in Santa Fe. The Kid knew that when the time was right, he would be aware of it.

Even though he was drawn to Diana Starbird, he wasn't going to take advantage of the hospitality she and her uncle had offered him. Conrad Browning might have tried to seduce her, at one time, because he'd been a bit of a self-centered scoundrel before making the acquaintance of his father, but Kid Morgan wouldn't.

He slid his gun back in its holster and stretched out on the bed. His intention was just to rest for a while, but he dozed off without meaning to.

The Kid came awake suddenly, and when he did, he had no idea how long he had been asleep. His dreams had been full of blood and death, of the anguished face of his wife and the leering, evil faces of the men who had kidnapped and killed her. The violent images of the deaths he had meted out to them in turn gave him no satisfaction. Blood paid for blood, but it never quite fulfilled the debt. As The Kid sat up in bed, he supposed that those all-too-vivid dreams had jolted him out of slumber.

Then he realized that somewhere outside, men shouted hoarsely and the roar of gunshots filled the air.

Chapter 8

As The Kid sprang out of bed, the Colt seemed to leap from the holster to his hand as if by magic. In the dimly lit room, no eye would have been able to follow his almost supernaturally swift movements. Gifted with the same sort of speed and accuracy with a gun that had made his father one of the deadliest gunfighters in the history of the West, Kid Morgan had honed those skills—skills he had never known he possessed until tragedy made them necessary—with long hours of practice.

He pushed the curtains aside at one of the windows and saw that shadows were gathering over the ranch headquarters. The sun was down, and twilight was settling in. It was one of the worst times of the day to try to see anything. The Kid spotted a couple of dark shapes lying huddled and motionless on the ground, and recognized them as men who were either wounded or dead.

Shots came from the barn, the bunkhouse, and

the house below him. The gunfire was directed at a stand of aspen trees about a hundred yards from the house. The Kid saw muzzle flashes stabbing through the darkness out there. He heard slugs thudding against the house.

The bushwhackers must have slipped in to the trees, then waited until dusk and opened fire on the ranch hands as they moved around on their final chores of the day. The Diamondback punchers would have scurried for cover, some of them reaching the barn, others the bunkhouse, maybe a few running in to the main house. The hidden riflemen continued pouring lead at the place, keeping the defenders pinned down.

It was impossible to know for sure how many bushwhackers were out there. The Kid estimated at least a dozen, judging by the muzzle flashes. Enough to do some damage, there was no doubt about that.

He couldn't shake the thought that Diana Starbird and her uncle were likely somewhere in the house, where a stray bullet could shatter a window or punch through a wall and find them.

He grimaced as his hand tightened on the Colt's grips. At that range, the six-gun wouldn't do him much good. He might be able to send his shots in a high enough arc that they would reach the trees, but there was no hope of any accuracy doing that.

What he needed were his Sharps and his Winchester.

Moving quickly, he holstered the revolver and

buckled the gun belt around his hips. He stomped his feet into his boots and pulled on his shirt. Leaving his hat where he'd hung it on the back of a chair, he left the room.

The house was in darkness. Either the lamps hadn't been lit yet, or someone had blown them all out. That was good. No sense giving the bushwhackers any better targets than they already had. The Kid clattered down the stairs to the big living room where he had talked with Diana and Captain Starbird earlier.

Someone who was crouched at one of the windows jerked around at the sound of his footsteps and exclaimed, "Son of a—" He recognized Diana's voice as she went on, "I almost shot you, Kid."

His eyes were adjusted enough to the dimness for him to be able to make out the rifle she clutched in her hands. "I'm glad you didn't," he said. "What's going on?"

"What does it sound like? We're under attack!"

"Malone and his men?"

"Bound to be. I guess he didn't figure you'd be here, so his word that he wouldn't try to kill you doesn't apply."

The Kid catfooted across the room to join her. As he crouched beside her, he asked, "Where's your uncle?"

"In his study. There are heavy shutters over the windows. He's safe."

"And I'll bet it's killing him to have to stay out of the fight, too," The Kid said.

"That's right. I didn't give him any choice, though. As soon as the shooting started, I pushed his chair in there and locked the door."

The Kid would have bet a hat that Diana was going to get a blistering earful from her uncle for doing that, once the fight was over. Assuming, of course, they both lived through it.

"You can get in there with him, if you want," she went on.

"Why would I do that?"

"You made it clear that our trouble with Malone isn't your fight," Diana said.

"I said I wasn't a hired gun. There's a difference." He started to get up.

She clutched his sleeve. "What are you doing?"

"I'm going to make a run for the barn. I need my Sharps and my Winchester."

"You're loco! You can't get to the barn. Those bastards'll shoot you full of holes if you try."

She didn't bother apologizing for her language, The Kid thought with a fleeting grin. He was in complete agreement with her. Bushwhackers *were* bastards.

"I don't like being shot at," he said. "It tends to make me want to shoot back."

"Well, you don't have to go to the barn to do it." She turned and waved a hand. "Your rifles are right over there on the table. One of the boys brought your gear in from the barn a little while ago, but I thought you might be asleep so I told him to just leave it all down here for now."

That was a lucky break, The Kid thought. He hurried over to the table and saw his Sharps and Winchester lying there. His saddlebags were draped over the back of a chair. He opened one of the pouches and reached inside to pull out a box of cartridges for the Sharps. After stuffing one pocket with ammunition, he filled another with Winchester rounds so they'd be handy. Then he draped the saddlebags over his shoulder.

"Where are you going?" Diana called as he started toward the stairs with a rifle in each hand.

"The high ground," he said. "The windows in my room have a good view of those trees."

He heard her rifle crack again as he headed up the stairs. He thought about telling her to keep her head down but didn't figure it would do any good.

When he reached his room, he tossed the saddlebags on the bed, then went to one of the windows and thrust the curtains all the way aside. Kneeling, he set the Winchester on the floor beside him and brought the heavy Sharps to his shoulder. It was already loaded. His thumb eased back the hammer, and he nestled his cheek against the smooth wood of the stock as he peered over the barrel at the trees where the bushwhackers had set up shop.

The Kid didn't have to wait very long, only a couple of heartbeats, before he saw a muzzle flash at just about the spot where he had the Sharps pointed. He shifted his aim just slightly and squeezed the trigger.

The boom of the heavy rifle filled the room and pounded against The Kid's ears, partially deafening him. Firing a Sharps in confined quarters was sort of like squatting under the barrel of a cannon as it went off.

He didn't have to be able to hear to do what he did next, though. He set the Sharps aside and snatched up the Winchester. Its magazine held fifteen rounds, with a sixteenth cartridge already in the chamber. He began firing, targeting the muzzle flashes he saw in the shadows under the trees.

The Kid's swift, deadly accurate fire from the second story window soon drew the attention of the bushwhackers. Bullets began to smack into the outer wall, and glass showered down around The Kid as more slugs shattered the upper panes of the window. As bullets whipped past his head, he threw himself backward out of the line of fire.

There was another window in the room and he rolled across the floor, avoiding the broken glass, and came up on one knee at that one. Gun flashes still winked like fireflies under the trees, but there were fewer of them. He had a hunch some of his shots had found their targets. He lined his sights and started firing again, emptying the Winchester in a long burst of well-placed shots.

There was no return barrage. The trees went dark as the bushwhackers stopped shooting. Morgan began reloading the Winchester and the Sharps while he had the chance. His ears were starting to work again and he heard Diana calling, "Hold your fire! Hold your fire!"

As the defenders' shots died away, The Kid leaned closer to the window and listened as intently as he could. The sound of rapid hoofbeats came to his ears.

Sam Rocklin shouted from the bunkhouse, "I think they're lightin' a shuck, Miss Diana!"

"Everyone hold your position!" Diana called back. "It could be a trick!"

The Kid was glad that she had some sense of strategy. It would help keep her from making any foolish mistakes.

He left the Sharps in the room but took the Winchester with him as he went downstairs. Diana heard him coming. She was waiting in the living room, along with a couple of ranch hands who had come in there from other parts of the house.

"Do you think they're really gone?" she asked.

The Kid said, "I don't know. It sounded like they were pulling out, but like you said, it could be a trick."

"If it is, we'll wait them out."

The Kid glanced at the window. Outside, the sky was almost completely dark. The stars would be putting in an appearance soon, if they weren't already. That darkness could come in handy.

"I'll go scout around and make sure they're gone."

He couldn't see Diana's face very well in the

gloom, but he heard the surprise in her voice as she said, "You can't do that. It's too dangerous."

"I'll be all right," The Kid assured her. "I know how to move without being seen and take care of myself if I run into any trouble." He thought briefly about his father, Frank Morgan. "I had a good teacher."

Grudgingly, Diana said, "All right . . . but be careful. Do you want some of the men to go with you?"

"No, I'll handle the chore by myself," The Kid answered without hesitation. He knew his own capabilities. He didn't know how quietly the other men could move.

He went to the back of the house, slipped out the rear door, and catfooted his way around the structure. As he worked his way around the bunkhouse and the barn toward the trees, he told himself to be especially cautious about not being seen. Some of the Diamondback hands might mistake him for one of the bushwhackers. Unfortunately, it was a risk he had to take.

He made it to the trees without incident and stopped in the thick shadows underneath them. His keen ears strained to hear any sound. The shooting had chased away any birds or small animals, so it was utterly quiet without the usual nocturnal stirrings and rustlings.

For a good five minutes, The Kid stood absolutely silent and motionless, barely breathing as he used his other senses in addition to his hearing.

He peered through the shadows, alert for even the slightest movement, and he smelled the thinning clouds of powdersmoke that lingered in the air and gradually faded. When he was convinced that the bushwhackers were actually gone, he stepped to the edge of the trees and called, "Hello, inside the house!"

"Mr. Morgan!" Diana's voice came back. "Are you all right?"

"They're gone," The Kid responded. "I'm coming out. Hold your fire."

"Hold your fire!" Diana echoed. "It's Mr. Morgan!"

The Kid walked out of the trees into the open, carrying the Winchester at his side. He noted that the dead or wounded cowboys he had seen lying on the ground earlier were gone and supposed that their friends had risked emerging from cover to pick them up.

He headed for the house, and by the time he got there and went up the steps, Diana was waiting on the porch with Sam Rocklin and some of the other men.

"The bushwhackers are gone," The Kid said. "If somebody will fetch a lantern, we can search the trees and see if they left any dead or wounded behind. I'd be willing to bet they didn't, though."

"Probably not," Diana agreed. "Malone wouldn't want to leave anybody behind who could testify against him." She turned to the foreman. "Sam, can you handle that?"

"I sure can," Rocklin replied with a curt nod. He turned to the other punchers and went on, "Orrie, fetch a lantern from the bunkhouse. Lon, you and Gordon come along, too."

The Kid started to turn around and accompany them, but Diana stopped him with a hand on his arm. "I wish you'd come with me, Kid," she said.

"To do what?"

"I have to let Uncle Owen out of the study . . . and I don't particularly want to be alone when I do it!"

Chapter 9

The Kid didn't really blame her for feeling that way. He knew that Owen Starbird would probably be furious at being shunted aside like that when danger threatened.

Diana led the way inside. "Do you think it's safe to light the lamps now?" she asked.

"I think so."

He heard the rasp of a match as Diana struck it against the stone hearth of the fireplace. Flame flared up. She held the match to the wick of a lamp that sat on the mantel, then lowered the chimney as it caught. Yellow, slightly flickering light spread out through the room.

Diana lit a lamp that she took from one of the tables, as well, then carried it with her as she opened a door that led to a hallway running toward the western end of the house. "Uncle Owen's study is down here," she explained.

As she approached a heavy door, she used her

free hand to reach in a pocket on her riding skirt and pull out a key. It rattled in the lock as she thrust it in and turned it. Leaving the key in the lock, she pulled the door open.

"It's bloody well about time," Owen Starbird's voice lashed out from the study. "I've been sitting in here in the dark listening to those shots, not knowing if you were alive or dead, damn it!" The wheels of his chair creaked as he shoved himself forward into the light. His stern face was taut with fury. "What happened?"

"Malone attacked the ranch," Diana said. "His men opened fire on the crew just as they were finishing the last of the day's work and coming in for supper. The men scattered and hunted cover, but a couple of them were wounded."

"Who?"

"Deuce Robinson and Jim Woodley."

"How badly are they hurt?"

Diana shook her head. "I don't know. The men carried them in to the bunkhouse. I sent Carmelita out there to take a look at them. We may have to send to Bristol for the doctor, though."

"Was anyone else injured?"

"A couple of bullet burns, that's all."

"And where are the bushwhackers now?"

"They took off for the tall and uncut." Diana glanced at The Kid. "I'd say Mr. Morgan tipped the odds in our favor when he opened fire on them from the second floor."

"I see." Starbird looked at The Kid and nodded.

"Thank you, sir. I greatly appreciate your assistance in this matter."

"They were shooting at me, too," The Kid pointed out.

Starbird smiled humorlessly. "And I suppose that makes it your fight."

"Damn right it does."

Starbird turned his gaze back to Diana again. "So the bushwhackers are gone, the wounded are being tended to, and the situation is under control?"

"That's right," she said.

The Kid wasn't surprised by what happened next. He could tell that Starbird had been holding in his anger until he found out exactly what had happened and what was going on. Satisfied that the emergency was over, the retired sea captain unleashed his fury in a blistering outburst.

"By the Lord Harry, girl, if you ever shove me in a room and lock the door as soon as trouble starts again, I'll see to it that you rue that day for the rest of your life!"

"I was trying to keep you from getting shot, damn it!" Diana flared back at him.

"I never hid from danger a single time in a long, perilous career. I always did my duty!"

"And what could you have done tonight?" Diana demanded. "In your condition, you can't—"

She stopped as her uncle's face turned white. The Kid had a feeling that Diana's words had just done more damage to Owen Starbird than a bullet could have.

A little lump of muscle moved around in Starbird's tightly clenched jaw. "You're right," he said. "I'm useless since my legs don't work anymore, aren't I?"

"That's not what I mean, Uncle Owen, and you know it."

"That's *exactly* what you meant. A man who can't walk isn't any good for anything. That's what you think. But you could have pushed me up to a window and given me a rifle. I can still shoot. My arms and my eyes work just fine."

"I thought of that," Diana admitted. "But you couldn't get out of the line of fire quickly if you needed to. It wasn't really a matter of what you can do, Uncle Owen. I just didn't want you to get hurt."

Her words actually made sense, The Kid thought, but they didn't seem to make any difference to Starbird. He just snorted in disgust, then said, "Tell Rocklin that I want him to take some of the men and trail those bushwhackers in the morning."

"What good will that do? We know Malone sent them."

"Yes, but if the trail leads back to the Trident, then we'll have proof we can turn over to the law."

"What law?" Diana asked. "Deputy Collier isn't going to try to arrest Malone by himself, and the Rangers don't care or they would have shown up in the valley by now. We have to handle this trouble ourselves."

"Tell Rocklin what I said anyway. I like to know where I stand before I act."

Diana nodded. "Of course. I don't think it's going to do any good, though."

Starbird started to wheel himself into the hall. "I want to know how those wounded men are doing. I'll get my crutches."

"That's not necessary," Diana told him. "I'll go out to the bunkhouse and check on them."

"I'd rather see for myself," Starbird said.

Diana glared at him for a second, then said, "Fine. Be stubborn if you want. I can't stop you."

"You most certainly can't." Starbird looked up at The Kid. "If I could prevail on you to give me a hand, Morgan . . ."

The Kid didn't want to get caught in the war of wills between Diana and her uncle. It seemed that he was in the middle, though, whether he wanted to be or not. Diana would probably see it as taking sides, but he stepped behind the wheelchair and gripped its handles as he said, "All right, Captain."

Sure enough, Diana glared at him. He ignored the look and pushed Starbird along the hall to the living room. Starbird's crutches leaned there against the wall. The Kid got them and brought them over, then helped Starbird stand up and get the crutches under his arms.

Diana followed them into the room and stood with her arms crossed and a look of disapproval on her face. The Kid glanced at her, then helped Starbird out the door and onto the porch. Getting down the steps wasn't easy, but with one of The Kid's hands on his arm to steady him, the retired naval officer managed. The two of them crossed the large open space between the main house and the bunkhouse.

The Kid matched his stride to Starbird's slow pace. He said, "I know it's none of my business, Captain, but—"

"How did I lose the use of my legs?" Starbird gave a short bark of hollow laughter. "You're right, it's none of your business, old boy. I don't blame you for being curious, though. You realize that a man couldn't captain one of Her Majesty's warships without being able to walk."

The Kid nodded. "Yes, that's the thought that crossed my mind."

"I began having trouble about three years ago. The doctors in England believed it was some sort of progressive nerve disorder, and they were right in that the condition steadily grew worse. That's why I had to retire from the Royal Navy, although I would have reached that age in a few more years anyway. My brother invited me to come here, to his ranch, rather than settling in England, and I accepted. To be honest, I'd spent so much time away from England over the years that I couldn't see returning there for good. It didn't really feel like home to me anymore. By the time I arrived in Texas and found that my brother was dead, I had to use two canes to get around, and my condition continued to worsen until my legs were no good to me at all. The muscles have wasted away since then. Carmelita tries to keep some life in them by massaging them every day, but it's a losing battle, I'm afraid."

"I'm sorry to hear that," The Kid said. "I appreciate you being honest with me. If I'm going to be in a fight, I like to know who my allies are."

Starbird looked over at him. "You sound as if you've reconsidered your earlier decision. Are you willing to work for us after all?"

"No, I'm still not looking for a job. I won't take your wages. But I didn't like Malone to start with, and after what happened tonight, I like him even less. Getting shot at makes it personal."

"Indeed. It's difficult to get much more personal than someone trying to kill you."

They reached the bunkhouse. Sam Rocklin stepped out to greet them. Light from inside the building spilled through the open door. "Cap'n," he said, "what can I do for you?"

"I came to check on the condition of the two lads who were wounded," Starbird replied.

The Kid could tell by the grim cast that came over Rocklin's face that the news wasn't good. "Jim Woodley's dead," the ramrod said. "He lost too much blood. There was nothin' Carmelita could do for him. Deuce is in pretty bad shape, but at least he's hangin' on for now."

"Would it help to fetch the doctor from Bristol, or should we take young Robinson into town?"

Rocklin shook his head. "I wouldn't move him.

The buckboard ride would finish him off, sure as shootin'. His best chance would be for somebody to bring the sawbones out here."

"Then send a rider now," Starbird ordered. "A man can reach the settlement by morning and have the doctor here before the day is over tomorrow."

"Yes, sir," Rocklin said with a nod. "I'll send Orrie. He's a good rider and has a fast hoss."

Starbird went on, "I already spoke to my niece about this, but since I'm out here, I might as well tell you myself. In the morning, I want you to take some men and trail those scoundrels who attacked the ranch. I want to know where they came from."

"Beggin' your pardon, Cap'n, but we know where they came from. Malone's spread."

Starbird shook his head. "We don't know that for a fact. I want confirmation."

"Well . . . you're the boss. When those varmints lit a shuck outta here, they were movin' pretty fast, so they weren't tryin' to cover their tracks. I bet they slowed down, though, after they put some ground behind 'em, and took care to make their trail harder to follow."

"Let's find out one way or the other, shall we?"

"You betcha." Rocklin inclined his head toward the interior of the bunkhouse. "You want to see Deuce?"

"Is he awake?"

"Off and on."

"Very well. Perhaps a word from me will lift the young man's spirits."

"That's what I was thinkin'."

Rocklin moved aside. Starbird thumped in to the bunkhouse on his crutches, followed by The Kid. Rocklin led them to one of the bunks, where Carmelita sat on a stool next to the bed and used a wet rag to wipe the forehead of the wounded man. That was probably all she could do for him. Bloody bandages were wrapped around the young cowboy's torso. At least the crimson stains didn't seem to be spreading, The Kid noted. Maybe the bleeding had stopped, which would be a good sign.

At the heavy sound of the captain's crutches, Deuce's eyes flickered open. He looked up and rasped, "C-Cap'n? Is that . . . you?"

"It is indeed, lad," Starbird replied. "I see that you've been wounded."

"It ain't . . . nothin' . . . Cap'n . . . I'll be . . . back on my feet . . . in no time . . . fightin' Black Terence and his . . . blasted skunks."

"I'm certain you will be. In the meantime, we'll give you the best possible care. Try to rest, and don't trouble your mind about anything."

The boy's eyelids started to slide closed, as if they weighed a hundred pounds each. "I'll try . . . Cap'n . . ."

Starbird frowned and leaned forward, balancing himself on the crutches. "I say! Is he—"

Carmelita shook her head and said, "He sleeps. That is all, Capitán."

"Very well." Starbird let go of one crutch, keeping it propped under his arm, and used that hand to pat the woman on the shoulder. "Do everything you can for him."

"Sí, Capitán."

As Starbird turned away from the bunk, he said to Rocklin, "Don't forget what I told you about tomorrow morning."

The foreman nodded. "Yes, sir. We'll get on the trail at first light."

The Kid spoke up. "I'm going with you."

Rocklin frowned. "I reckon that's up to the cap'n."

"Mr. Morgan was of invaluable assistance tonight," Starbird said. "I see no harm in him accompanying you, Sam."

"Sure, boss, whatever you say." Rocklin hesitated. "Earlier, though, before all the shootin' broke out, I was talkin' to some of the boys. They've heard of this fella. Seems he's gettin' quite a rep as a gunfighter."

Starbird smiled. "Then it sounds as if Mr. Morgan is exactly the sort of chap we need on our side, doesn't it?"

Chapter 10

By the time The Kid and Captain Starbird got back to the main house, Diana had rustled up some supper since Carmelita was busy in the bunkhouse, taking care of the wounded Deuce Robinson. It was a simple meal, leftover beef, beans, and tortillas, but it tasted good to The Kid, especially when it was washed down with strong coffee.

After supper, Starbird asked The Kid to help him get ready for bed, another chore Carmelita usually handled. Diana offered to help, but Starbird shook his head firmly.

"Wouldn't be proper, don't you know," he said in a tone that didn't allow for any argument. "Dashed *im*proper, in fact."

"I don't mind," The Kid said. He assisted Starbird to the captain's bedroom, which was on the first floor for the sake of convenience, across the hall from his study.

Once there, The Kid helped with the necessary

tasks, carrying them out with no fuss or extra delay. He knew it had to be galling to a man as proud as Owen Starbird to need a helping hand with such basic, private matters.

"Thank you, old boy," Starbird said from the big, four-poster bed when The Kid was ready to leave the room. "I believe we're fortunate that my niece happened to run into you." He hesitated. "You strike me as a man with a kind heart."

The Kid chuckled. "I haven't been accused of that too often. I'm a gunfighter, remember?"

"That doesn't mean you can't be a decent individual as well."

"Most folks would disagree with you about that," The Kid said with a smile.

He lifted a hand in farewell as he went out of the room. After easing the door closed behind him, he went back along the hall to the living room, which also served as the dining room. Diana still sat at the table, sipping from her coffee cup.

"There's brandy, if you'd like some," she said without looking at him.

"That's a mighty tempting offer."

She nodded toward the sideboard. "Help yourself."

The Kid went over and poured brandy from a crystal decanter into a glass. He asked Diana, "How about you?"

She smiled and held up her cup. "You don't think this is all coffee in here, do you?"

He returned the smile and sipped the brandy. It

was excellent, much better than what he expected to find on a cattle ranch in an isolated West Texas valley.

"I got your uncle settled in for the night," he said.

"Thank you. Sometimes Uncle Owen isn't the easiest person in the world to deal with . . . but I'm sure he'd say the same thing about me!"

"I won't pretend to know him very well after just meeting him, but he strikes me as a proud man. It must be difficult for him to accept being crippled."

Diana's expression softened into one of sympathy and even a little pity, which The Kid was sure Owen Starbird would hate if he saw it.

"If he hadn't already been sick when he came here, and if my father was still alive, Malone never would have tried anything. He wouldn't have dared to go up against the Starbird brothers." She took a bigger slug of the brandy-laced coffee. "But my father is gone, and Uncle Owen is just a shadow of the man he used to be. Life just isn't fair."

The Kid thought about some of the tragedies that had dogged his own life, beginning with the murder of his mother by outlaws and the similar circumstances that had taken his wife Rebel's life. He said, "It never claimed to be fair." After a moment, he went on, "I talked to your uncle about what happened to him. The doctors here and over in England weren't able to do anything for him at all?"

Diana shook her head. "They just told him he'd have to resign himself to the fact that he'd never walk properly again. By now, of course, his legs have weakened so much that I don't think he'll ever walk again, period. At least, not without his crutches."

"That's a terrible thing, but at least he's still alive."

"If you can call it living, for a man like Uncle Owen who led such an active existence."

The Kid tossed back the rest of his drink. He wasn't the sort to sit around and mope about his own bad luck, or anyone else's for that matter.

"Your uncle already talked to Sam Rocklin about trying to trail those bushwhackers in the morning. We'll be riding out at first light."

Diana's eyebrows rose. "You're going with them?"

"I know a little about tracking," he said. He wasn't as good at it as his father was, but he wouldn't hold the group back and might even be able to help. If they happened to run into more trouble, his guns would definitely come in handy.

"So you're really in this fight now," Diana said as she looked intently at him.

"It appears that I am."

"Because Malone shot at you."

The Kid set the empty glass on the sideboard. "I don't like to let anybody get away with that."

"But after the fight with Wolfram you were still willing to ride away."

"That particular fight was over," The Kid said with a shrug. "It was Malone's idea to start another one."

Diana shook her head and said, "I'll never understand men. If you and Uncle Owen are prime examples, then you're all stubborn, bullheaded, and impossible to figure out!"

"Sort of like women," The Kid said.

Then he headed upstairs before Diana could think of anything to say in return. As he climbed the stairs, he couldn't help but wonder if he really was looking for trouble after all, despite telling himself that he wasn't.

Otherwise, why did he keep winding up in the middle of it?

Carmelita was in the kitchen when The Kid came down the next morning before dawn. Thankfully his dreams had not been haunted by nightmarish memories.

"How's that young cowboy Deuce?" he asked Carmelita as she stood at the stove preparing flapjacks. A pot of coffee was brewing and smelled good.

"Señor Deuce is still alive," she replied. "That is the best one can say, when he was shot like that. *Tres* bullets, they go right through him."

Carmelita was speaking English all right that morning, The Kid noticed. He didn't say anything about her apparent inability to understand the language the night before when he asked her about Owen Starbird's condition.

"It's better that the bullets went on through," he

commented. "That way the doctor won't have to dig them out when he gets here."

Carmelita nodded. "Sí. If they did not do too much damage, and if Señor Deuce did not lose too much blood, perhaps he will recover." She put some of the flapjacks onto a plate, turned and placed it on the table. "Sit. Eat. I will pour coffee."

The Kid did as he was told, looking down to hide the quick grin that flashed across his face at Carmelita's no-nonsense tone. "Do you cook for the hands, too?" he asked.

The woman shook her head. "No, only for El Capitán and Señorita Diana, and for Señor Rocklin when he joins them. There is an old *hombre* who cooks for the *vaqueros*. He used to be one of them, a cowboy. I also clean the house and care for El Capitán."

"Yes, I got the feeling from talking to him that he's very grateful for your help."

A snort came from Carmelita. "That one would never say such a thing, not to one such as me. A servant."

The conversation was edging into areas where The Kid didn't want to go. Other people's emotions were their business. He picked up a fork, poured syrup on the flapjacks, and dug in. The food was excellent. A few minutes later, Carmelita added some bacon onto his plate, and the meal got even better. The Kid didn't have to fake a hearty appetite and an appreciation for what he was eating.

Diana came into the kitchen, dressed in the same sort of riding outfit she had worn the day before, but gray instead of brown. The Kid started to get to his feet, but she waved him back into his chair.

"We don't stand on ceremony around here, Kid," she said. "Carmelita, I'm ready for some of your coffee, and that food smells mighty good."

"I wasn't sure I'd see you up this early," The Kid commented as Diana sat down at the table with him and Carmelita placed breakfast in front of her.

"Rocklin said we were riding out after those bushwhackers at first light, didn't he?"

The Kid frowned. "Yes, but I didn't know you were going along."

"I don't like being shot at any more than you do, Kid, and it was worse for me because I was attacked in my own home. I'm not going to let Malone get away with that."

"If we run into trouble, somebody could get hurt trying to watch out for you."

Diana's coffee cup rattled against its saucer as she put it down with a little more force than was necessary. "Nobody has to *watch out* for me, as you put it," she snapped. "I'm perfectly capable of taking care of myself. You've seen with your own eyes that I'm a good shot with a rifle, and I ride as well or better than half the men who work for Diamondback."

The Kid didn't doubt that, but he didn't like the idea of Diana going along. It was potentially dangerous. She was half-owner of the ranch, though, so it was her choice to make.

"All right," he said, "but if the bullets start to fly, I'm going to be looking to save my hide before I am yours."

"Fine. That's exactly the way I want it."

Even as The Kid made the declaration, he knew that probably wasn't the way things would work out. In the event of trouble, his instincts would force him to protect Diana. He wasn't going to admit that to her.

By the time they finished breakfast and left the big house, the eastern sky was gray, with a band of orange along the horizon that signaled the approach of dawn. The Kid took along his Sharps and Winchester. Diana carried her saddle gun, the same carbine she had used to blast the rattlesnake the day before.

Sam Rocklin and four other men were in the corral, cutting out their horses from the remuda. Rocklin saw Diana walking alongside The Kid and swore. He came over to the corral fence and said, "Miss Diana, what're you thinkin' about doin'?"

"I'm coming with you," she said. "This is Starbird range, and one of the Starbirds needs to help find out who attacked it."

"I know what you're sayin', but I ain't sure it's a good idea for you to ride with us. Could be some trouble."

"I hope so," Diana said. "That would mean we've found the men we're looking for."

Rocklin scratched his beard-stubbled jaw. "I reckon you could look at it like that . . ." he began.

"It won't do any good to argue. I own half this ranch, you know."

"Yeah, but your uncle calls the shots most of the time, and he leaves most of the decisions up to me."

"I'm coming along, and that's final," Diana said.

Rocklin sighed. "All right. We'll get your horse saddled and ready to ride."

"I can saddle my own horse."

"Yes'm. Whatever you want."

Rocklin didn't look or sound happy about the prospect of Diana going with them, but clearly, he knew that arguing with her was pointless. Probably he had tried and failed at that little chore in the past, The Kid thought.

The buckskin was in one of the stalls in the barn, rather than the corral. The Kid saddled the rangy stallion and slid both long guns into their sheaths. He attached the saddlebags and led the buckskin out of the barn, past the stall where Diana was tightening the cinches on her chestnut's saddle. She came out of the barn only a minute or so behind him.

Rocklin and the other hands had their mounts ready as well and had gathered in front of the barn. All five of them were armed with pistols and rifles. They would be a formidable little group, able to handle most trouble they were likely to run into.

If they encountered a large group of Malone's hired guns, they would be outnumbered. But The Kid figured Rocklin didn't want to take the rest of the crew along and leave Diamondback undefended, especially since they were shorthanded.

"How's Deuce?" Diana asked as they all mounted up.

"Seems a mite stronger this mornin'," Rocklin said. "He was able to sleep some durin' the night without the pain botherin' him too much."

"That's good. Orrie should be back from Bristol with the doctor sometime today. With any luck, Deuce will pull through."

"Yes'm."

"Also with any luck, we'll catch up to the men who shot him."

Rocklin nodded grimly. The Kid wasn't sure if the foreman would consider that lucky or not, since Diana was coming with them.

The other cowboys looked uneasy, too. The Kid knew that Diana had a lot of pride and just wanted to help out, wanted to step forward and grasp the reins of power like her father or her uncle would have done if they'd been able to. He could understand that, maybe even sympathize with it, but he also knew that these rough-and-tumble cowboys would never really be comfortable about having a lady riding with them after bushwhackers, even a lady boss. Maybe *especially* a lady boss.

Diana nodded to Rocklin. "All right, Sam."

Rocklin sighed and said, "Yes'm." He lifted a hand and waved it forward as the bright orange sphere that was the sun began to rise over the desert to the east. "Let's ride!"

Chapter 11

Starting out, they rode only to the trees where the riflemen had hidden to open fire on the ranch. There, in the orange light that began to flood over the valley, they searched for any signs left behind by the bushwhackers.

It didn't take a skilled tracker to see the mounds of droppings and the muddle of tracks that marked the place where someone had held the horses. To the experienced eye, the prints left by the horseshoes were distinct enough from each other so that a close scrutiny of them allowed Rocklin to say, "I make it fourteen horses, give or take one."

"That means if we catch up to 'em, they'll outnumber us two to one, Sam," one of the punchers pointed out.

"Yeah, but maybe they ain't all together anymore," Rocklin said. "Anyway, the boss didn't order us to track those bushwhackers down and shoot it out with 'em. He just wants us to find out where they came from."

Another cowboy snorted. "Shoot, we know that already! They were Malone's men!"

Diana spoke up. "I had the same conversation with Uncle Owen. He wants proof."

That ended the discussion. The members of the group went back to studying the ground under the trees. They found a number of cartridges that had been ejected from Winchesters, as well as the butts of a few quirlies, but nothing else. Certainly nothing that would positively identify the men who had opened fire on the ranch headquarters.

The Kid saw where the tracks led away from the trees. The trail ran straight south toward the Severn River. As Rocklin had predicted, when the gunmen fled, they didn't try to cover their tracks. All they'd been interested in was putting some distance between themselves and Diamondback.

As the riders set out to follow the trail, The Kid asked Rocklin, "Where's Malone's spread located?"

"Well south of the river, mostly along the hills that border the valley on that side. But one of the ranches he picked up cheap when the owner wanted to sell out was called the Arrowhead, because of the way it's shaped. That range comes to a point at the river itself, and the wedge it forms extends across the road. That's why Malone got the idea he could dictate who comes and who goes in the valley. About a quarter mile of the main trail through Rattlesnake Valley cuts through his range."

The Kid shook his head. "That won't stand up legally . . . but I suppose Malone isn't the sort of man who worries too much about things like that, is he?"

"You got that right, Morgan. Malone don't care about nothin' except gettin' what he wants."

As Rocklin spoke, his eyes cut over toward Diana, who was riding on his other side. The Kid noticed that glance and remembered what Diana had said about Malone wanting to marry her as part of his plan to get revenge on her uncle. Obviously Rocklin knew about that, and the rest of the men probably did, too. Malone didn't strike The Kid as the sort of hombre who would bother to keep his plans a deep, dark secret.

They followed the tracks to the river. There was no ford there, but from the looks of it, the fleeing bushwhackers had put their horses into the water and made the animals swim across.

"It ain't far to the ford," Rocklin said. "It's only about half a mile downstream. We'll cross down yonder, then double back to pick up the trail."

"It would save time to swim the horses across here," Diana pointed out.

Rocklin nodded. "Yes'm, it would, but it'd be more dangerous, too."

"What would you do if I wasn't along?" Diana

demanded. "Would you still go downstream to the ford? Or are you just trying to protect me?"

Rocklin looked uncomfortable, so The Kid suspected he knew what the foreman's answer was. As Rocklin hesitated, The Kid spoke up.

"It's not like we're hot on their trail," he said. "They came through here more than twelve hours ago. Taking an extra half hour to cross where it's safer won't have any effect on the tracks."

"I suppose you're right," Diana said, "but I don't like being coddled."

"I think we've all got that idea," The Kid said, ignoring the angry glare she gave him in return. He didn't work for her, so he could afford to speak his mind.

The riders turned and headed downstream along the grassy riverbank. They had only gone about fifty yards when a pair of sharp cracks sounded. The Kid recognized them instantly as rifle shots, even as he heard the ugly sound of lead smacking into flesh, followed hard by grunts of pain.

The shots had come from the other side of the river. As the Diamondback hands began to shout, The Kid wheeled his horse and pulled the Winchester from its sheath. Another shot blasted from a line of trees across the river, and this time a cowboy's hat leaped from his head as a bullet ventilated it. The Kid whipped the rifle to his shoulder. He sprayed lead into the trees five times, firing as fast as he could work the Winchester's lever.

The Kid's reaction was the swiftest, but as the shots from his rifle rolled out, the other members of the group began to fight back. Six-shooters blasted, and some of the men got their rifles into play, as well.

Even in the middle of the fight, The Kid's brain was working. He suspected that the bushwhackers from the night before had left a couple of men behind to see if anyone tried to follow their trail. That was the only explanation that made any sense.

After a few loud, frantic moments, Sam Rocklin bellowed, "Hold your fire! Hold your fire!"

The Kid knew why Rocklin issued that order. He hadn't heard any more shots from across the river for several seconds. It was likely that the two men over there had taken a few potshots, then fled. Unless, of course, the speedy response from The Kid and his companions had tagged the bush-whackers.

Rocklin waved his men toward some nearby rocks. "Take cover and keep your heads down until I see what's over there!" he ordered. "Tend to the fellas who got hit!"

The Kid saw two men sagging in their saddles. They'd been wounded in the opening volley, and while neither man had been knocked off his horse, they could still be seriously injured.

As Rocklin put his horse into the water, Diana tried to follow him. The Kid moved so that his buckskin blocked her.

"Get in the rocks with the others," he told her. "I'll go with Rocklin."

"Damn it, you can't order me around!" she blazed at him.

He leaned over in the saddle and jerked her reins out of her hands. "I'll take you in there and make you stay," he threatened, "but if I do that, Rocklin may have to face those bushwhackers alone."

She glared at him for a second, then burst out, "Oh, all right, blast it! But I'm not going to forget this, Kid."

He didn't let go of the reins. "Word of honor you'll get behind those rocks?"

"Word of honor," Diana grated out.

The Kid nodded and released her reins. He swung the buckskin around and heeled the horse into motion. The buckskin lunged into the river, and in a moment the water was deep enough so that he had to start swimming.

Because he believed the men left behind by the bushwhackers had fled, The Kid didn't expect any more shots to come from the trees. But he couldn't keep from steeling his muscles for the impact of a bullet anyway as he followed Rocklin across the river.

When they reached the far side of the stream, the horses splashed up the bank. Rocklin was in front, but The Kid urged the buckskin alongside the ramrod's mount. They rode about twenty feet apart as they entered the trees. The Kid guided his horse with his knees and held the Winchester in both hands, ready to fire at a second's notice.

His keen eyes searched the sun-dappled shadows under the trees but saw no signs of movement. Once again, the shooting had driven off any birds or small animals, so the area was quiet except for the thudding of hoofbeats as The Kid and Rocklin rode around. After several minutes, Rocklin called, "They must've lit a shuck. They ain't here no more."

"That's what it looks like to me, too," The Kid agreed.

Rocklin dismounted to take a closer look at the ground. The Kid followed suit. Rocklin found some tracks and pointed at them, saying, "Look here. I recognize the big nick on that horseshoe. It belongs to one of the hosses we been trailin'."

The Kid nodded. "Proof that these two bushwhackers were part of the same bunch."

"I never doubted that."

"Neither did I, but as Captain Starbird pointed out, it's good to have proof." The Kid used the barrel of his rifle to push aside some brush and went on, "Look at this, Sam."

Rocklin leaned over and craned his neck to see what The Kid was talking about. He grunted as he saw the splash of dark red blood on the ground.

"Reckon we must've winged one of the skalleyhooters."

The Kid said, "Yes, and from the looks of that

blood, it might've been a serious injury. We know we did some damage, anyway."

"It ain't enough," Rocklin replied grimly. "It ain't gonna be enough until Malone and his whole crew of gun-wolves are dead."

"Is that what you want? An all-out war?"

Rocklin glared. "Malone called the tune at this here ball. He can damn well dance to it."

The Kid couldn't argue with that. The results of a man's actions were on his own head. Trying to make out that a person wasn't responsible for what he or she did in life was just crazy as far as The Kid was concerned.

Two sets of hoofprints led away from the trees, headed south. That came as no surprise to The Kid. He and Rocklin stepped out of the trees onto the bank and waved their rifles over their heads, knowing that the men forted up in the rocks would see them. A moment later, Diana and one of the Diamondback hands emerged from the rocks.

Rocklin cupped his hands around his mouth and shouted across the stream, "They're gone! Go on down to the ford and meet us there!"

The cowhand called back, "Junior Pettigrew's hurt pretty bad, Sam, and Ned Lunsford's got a bullet hole in his leg!"

"Can Ned ride?"

"Yeah, I expect he can!"

"Put Junior on his horse, and Ned can take him back to the ranch!" Rocklin ordered.

The cowboy nodded and waved a hand to indicate that he understood. He and Diana disappeared back into the rocks. The Kid and Rocklin mounted up but waited on the riverbank until the entire group came in sight again. The two wounded men, riding double, started back toward Diamondback. Diana and the other two punchers followed the north bank of the Severn toward the ford.

"There are only five of us now," Rocklin pointed out as he and The Kid started along the south bank. "The odds against us if we run into more trouble just got a mite higher. That damn pirate's whittlin' us down."

"That may be exactly what he's trying to do," The Kid said. "He knows he can't stand up to your outfit in open combat, so he's going to employ guerrilla tactics against Diamondback."

"It ain't no fair way to fight," Rocklin complained.

"That's because men like Malone don't care about being fair. They want to win no matter the cost."

Chapter 12

A few minutes later, The Kid and Rocklin rendezvoused with Diana and the other two punchers at the ford. Diana and her two companions, Nick Weaver and Carl Addams, crossed the river and reined in as they emerged from the water.

"Did you find anything in those trees?" Diana asked.

"Some blood," Rocklin answered. "Looked like we ventilated one of 'em."

"Good," Diana said with a note of fierce satisfaction in her voice. "I hope the bastard bleeds to death." She looked around at the men. "And I don't care how unladylike that is!"

"Nobody said anything," The Kid drawled as he lifted his reins. "Come on, let's try to pick up that trail again."

They rode upstream, and when they reached the trees where the riflemen had hidden for the most recent ambush attempt, Rocklin said, "Nick, you and Carl follow these two fellas. Miss Starbird and Mr. Morgan and I will pick up that other trail. I'm bettin' they'll meet up before too long."

"Are you sure that splitting such a small force is a good idea, Sam?" Diana asked.

"The boss wants to know as much as we can tell him about the varmints who attacked the ranch, ma'am. Because of those tracks, I'm convinced the two men who opened fire on us a little while ago were part of the same bunch that attacked Diamondback yesterday evenin', but your uncle would want to know for sure."

Diana thought it over for a second and then nodded. "You're right. We'll split up, but it won't be for long."

"That's what I'm thinkin'. Anyway, we'll still all be within shoutin' distance of each other. We may not even be out of sight."

That turned out to be the case, but not for the reasons the foreman probably thought. The Kid, Diana, and Rocklin rode along the river until they came to a spot opposite the place where the men who had raided the ranch put their horses into the stream. There were no tracks on the bank to show where the bushwhackers had emerged.

"This ain't good," Rocklin said with a frown. "I know we're in the right place. I took note of that dead limb in that tree over yonder." He pointed across the river to a tree on the northern bank. "The trail they left ran right past it."

"They didn't swim their horses straight across,"

The Kid speculated. "They went upstream or more likely downstream for a ways before they came out of the water. Like you said, Sam, at first they were just trying to get away, but then they started trying to cover their tracks."

"And they done a good job of it, too, dang it."

Diana suggested, "Why don't we just ride up and down the river until we find where they came out. They couldn't have gone *too* far."

Rocklin scratched his jaw as he thought about it. "Might be better to follow those other tracks with Nick and Carl," he decided. "They're bound to join up with the others sooner or later."

The Kid wasn't so sure of that. If Black Terence Malone was any sort of strategist, he might have ordered the men he left behind *not* to rejoin the rest of the bunch. In fact, they might have all split up, leaving the river at different spots, one by one, so that their tracks would be easier to conceal.

The Kid suddenly had a hunch that they wouldn't be able to prove the men who'd attacked Diamondback the previous evening were from Malone's Trident ranch.

He and Diana and Rocklin rode back to rejoin Weaver and Addams. Together, they followed the tracks left by the two men who had taken those potshots at them. After a quarter mile, the hoofprints reached the main road through Rattlesnake Valley. It appeared that no one else had used the road that morning, because Rocklin was able to tell that the two riders turned east, toward the settlement of Bristol.

"Looks like they ain't headin' for Malone's spread after all," Rocklin said.

"That doesn't mean anything," Diana snapped. "They could work for him anyway."

The Kid knew she was right about that, but since the trail didn't lead to the Trident, they couldn't prove it.

"I hate to go back to the ranch and tell your uncle we failed," Rocklin said, "but I don't see what else we can do. Anyway, I don't want to leave the crew shorthanded any longer'n we have to. Malone might try something else."

The Kid rested his hands on the saddlehorn and said, "There's one more thing we can do . . . or rather, that I can do. I'll ride on to the settlement and take a look around. Maybe the man we wounded went looking for the doctor, and I can get a line on him that way."

"Hmm," Rocklin said as he thought over the suggestion. "Maybe. But Doc Eggars ought to be well on his way out to Diamondback by now to have a look at Deuce."

"The wounded man wouldn't know that," The Kid pointed out.

Diana said, "I think it's a good idea. I'm coming with you, Kid."

He shook his head. "No."

"What do you mean, no?" she shot back at him. "Don't you know by now that you can't tell me what to do?"

"I'm saying it wouldn't be a smart thing to

do," The Kid explained. "Malone may have his suspicions that I've thrown in with you, but he can't be sure of that. Most of the people in town won't have any idea who I am. If you and I ride in together, everyone in Bristol will know that I'm connected to your ranch. That's liable to make it harder for me to find out anything. Didn't your uncle say that the citizens weren't as sympathetic to Diamondback as they used to be?"

"That's right," Diana admitted with a touch of bitterness in her voice. "The ones who have been there the longest seem to have forgotten how much my father did for this valley, and the people who've arrived more recently don't know and don't care." She paused, then added, "There are times when I think that progress and civilization aren't always such good things."

The Kid didn't say anything, but he agreed with her on that score, even though for most of his life he had been a blatant representative of civilization's steady march across the West.

"All right," she went on. "I understand what you're getting at, Kid. I'll go back to the ranch with Sam and the others. Just be careful. Malone could have spies in town."

The Kid nodded. "I'm always careful," he said. He'd had to be, in order to survive the past tumultuous year.

Diana turned her horse and rode back toward the ford with Rocklin and the other men. She hipped around in the saddle before they went out of sight and looked back at The Kid with a peculiar intensity for a few seconds. He felt her eyes on him and knew she was torn in her feelings. Her pride and stubbornness led her to argue with him at nearly every turn, and yet he knew that she was drawn to him. Under different circumstances, he might have felt the same way about her.

But she reminded him too much of Rebel, another beautiful young woman born and raised on the frontier and blessed with the same sort of headlong recklessness and stubborn determination that Diana possessed.

And that terrible wound in Kid Morgan's heart caused by Rebel's loss was still too fresh, too raw.

It was easy to find the settlement. All he had to do was follow the road. By midday, he rounded a bend in the trail as it curved around a hill and saw Bristol laid out before him.

At first glance it appeared to be a typical West Texas cowtown with false-fronted businesses along both sides of a main street that stretched for several blocks and a mixture of frame and adobe residences on the cross streets. But a closer look revealed that there were a number of more substantial buildings, too, including a two story red brick structure. The Kid wouldn't be surprised if it housed the local bank, along with maybe some lawyers' offices and things like that. As he rode closer, he saw that a few of the frame buildings had actual second stories, not just false fronts. One of them sported a large, colorful sign, and as The Kid rode closer, he was able to make out the words RATTLER'S DEN SALOON. The sign had a drawing of a rattlesnake coiled and ready to strike, he saw as he entered the main street on the buckskin.

The hitch rails in front of the saloon were full, and there were a lot of horses and wagons tied up in other places along the street. Sam Rocklin had pointed out that one of the men who'd shot at them earlier was riding a mount with a large nick out of the horseshoe on its front left hoof. The Kid couldn't pick that particular print out of the welter of hoofprints in the street, though, so short of going along and checking the shoes on every horse he came to, he didn't see how that knowledge was going to help him. He couldn't very well do that if he wanted to blend in.

He angled the buckskin toward the Rattler's Den, thinking that the biggest, busiest saloon in town was usually a good place to pick up information.

The Kid swung down from the saddle and found a place at the crowded hitch rail to loop the reins. A plank porch ran in front of the saloon, which took up more than half a block. A saddlemaker's shop had the rest of the frontage on Main Street in the block. The Kid stepped onto the porch and started toward the batwings.

They swung out suddenly, just before he reached them, and he stepped back quickly to avoid being hit by them.

Two men pushed onto the boardwalk, one of them laughing at an obscene comment made by the other about a girl who worked in the saloon. They stopped short at the sight of The Kid, and a man with an eagle's beak of a nose and a droopy black mustache growled, "Watch where you're goin', mister."

"I was," The Kid said. "That's why I was able to keep the two of you from running into me."

The second man glared at him. "He's got a smart mouth on him, Breck." Like his companion, the man was tall and brawny, with a shock of rusty hair under a pushed-back Stetson. "You reckon we oughta teach him some manners?"

"Naw, he's just some damn stupid dude, Early," Breck said. "We ain't got time to fool with him."

He started past The Kid, who stood his ground and didn't get out of the way. Breck's shoulder rammed hard into his. It was clear from the man's attitude that he thought he could brush The Kid aside easily, but that wasn't how it worked out. Instead, the deceptive strength in The Kid's rangy body caused Breck to stumble to the side.

"What the hell!" the redheaded Early howled. "Did you see what he done?"

Breck caught himself and said, "Yeah, I saw." His upper lip curled in a snarl. "Stranger, are you lookin' for trouble?"

"I never go looking for trouble," The Kid said out of habit, even though he had started to doubt that, "but I don't back down from it."

"Seems to me like you're cravin' it, and we're just the hombres to give it to you."

The Kid wondered if those two men were the ones who had shot at him and Diana and the others earlier in the day. They might have spotted him through one of the saloon's front windows and recognized him, then staged the confrontation so they would have an excuse for killing him. Both men sported six-guns in tied-down holsters. If they made a play, The Kid figured he would have to kill both of them. There wouldn't be time for anything fancy. But he didn't particularly want them dead, in case there was anything he could learn from them.

So he said to Breck, "I think you're the one who's hunting trouble, mister," and to prove it, he brought his left fist up with blinding speed and slammed a punch right onto the man's beaklike nose.

Chapter 13

The blow landed cleanly, with all the strength The Kid could put behind it. Taken by surprise, Breck hadn't even tried to block it. As the punch exploded on his nose, the impact sent him flying backward to crash into the wall of the saloon.

A surprised and outraged Early yelled, "Hey!", but he didn't reach for his gun. Instead he lunged at The Kid, swinging a big fist in a roundhouse blow.

The Kid ducked under the sweeping punch and bored in, hooking a hard right then a left into Early's midsection. One after the other, his fists buried themselves in the man's belly. Foul, whiskey-laden breath gusted out of Early's mouth as he groaned and doubled over in pain.

That put him in position for the uppercut that might have finished him off if The Kid had gotten the chance to throw it. Instead, Breck recovered his balance without falling and launched himself at The

Kid in a diving tackle. His brawny arms wrapped around The Kid's waist. Both men hit the railing along the edge of the porch. It broke with a loud, splintering crack, and they sailed off the planks into the street.

The Kid hit the dirt first, with Breck landing heavily on top of him. Pain shot through him, and for a second he thought that the man's crushing weight had broken his ribs. It drove the air out of his lungs, that was for sure. Stunned, breathless, and in pain, for a second all The Kid could do was lie there while Breck hammered at him.

"Lemme at him, Breck!" Early shouted. "I'll stomp the hell outta him!"

The words penetrated The Kid's brain and brought a sense of urgency back to him. He knew that the two hard cases were perfectly capable of stomping and kicking him to death if they got the chance. The lone deputy in Bristol probably wouldn't interfere against two-to-one odds, even if he knew what was going on in front of the Rattler's Den, which he might not. The Kid couldn't expect any help from anyone else in the settlement, either. Nobody there knew him.

That was why he was surprised when he heard the sudden boom of a shot, and a husky voice ordering, "All right, get the hell away from him, or the next one goes in your head, Breck! The same goes for you, Early! Stay back!"

The Kid was still shaken up, but his brain had started working again well enough for him to realize that the voice belonged to a woman. He didn't know why she had stepped in to help him, but at least Breck wasn't walloping him anymore. He was mighty grateful for that.

"You better put that gun down, Sophia," Breck said with a thunderous frown as he looked up at the boardwalk in front of the saloon. "It's liable to go off."

"It'll go off, all right," the woman said. The Kid twisted his head, but he couldn't quite see her. Breck's bulky form blocked his view. She went on, "It'll splatter your brains all over the street."

Muttering curses, Breck pushed himself off The Kid. He got to his feet and stepped back. "I don't take kindly to bein' threatened," he blustered, "especially by a woman."

"Yeah!" Early added. "You can't tell us what to do, Sophia. You ain't our boss."

"Yes, well, if I was desperate enough to hire troublemaking oafs like the two of you, I wouldn't be much of a businesswoman, now would I?"

The two men frowned, not having a comeback for that.

The Kid rolled onto his side, then onto his belly so he could get his hands and knees under him and push himself up. He grabbed his hat out of the dusty street as he came to his feet.

The woman who stood on the porch held a Colt Navy revolver in her right hand and steadied her grip with her left hand on that wrist. The gun didn't waver a bit as she pointed it at Breck and Early.

She was a real beauty, The Kid saw, despite the rather garish getup she wore. A large purple plume of some sort stuck up from the bun of rich brown hair gathered at the back of her head. She wore a purple gown that left her arms and much of her shoulders bare. A couple of thin straps held it up. The neck was cut low enough to reveal the swell of her rounded breasts, and the waist nipped in before flaring out to emphasize the curve of her hips. The outfit was tight enough and revealing enough that The Kid wondered where she kept the Colt.

"You two have had your fun," Sophia went on. "Go on wherever you were headed when you left. I don't want to see you back here for at least a week."

Breck burst out, "Damn it, Sophia, you can't do that! You got the best liquor in the valley!"

A thin smile curved her full red lips. "That's right. Maybe if you get thirsty enough, you boys will remember not to start another brawl in front of my place. Look at that railing! Tell your boss I'll send him the bill after I have it repaired."

"Malone ain't gonna like that," Early complained.

"I don't give a damn what Black Terence Malone likes or doesn't like," Sophia snapped. "You boys tell him what I said. Now get out of here!"

Scowling, the two men turned toward the hitch rack. The beautiful Sophia had confirmed The

Kid's hunch. Breck and Early worked for Malone, and he was more convinced than ever that they were the bushwhackers from the river, even though neither of them appeared to be wounded.

As they jerked the reins of their horses loose and swung up in to their saddles, The Kid used his hat to slap dust from his trousers and moved closer. He wanted to get a look at the hoofprints their horses left. If one of them sported a nick in the shoe, that was the last bit of proof he'd need.

"Stay back, stranger," Sophia warned him sharply. "Don't go starting up that fight again after I already saved your bacon once."

"Don't worry, I'm not starting anything," The Kid assured her. He brushed dust from his hat and clapped it on his head, and as he did, Breck and Early turned their horses and rode off at a gallop, causing dust to swirl in the air behind them.

That didn't keep The Kid from checking out the hoofprints. His forehead creased. Neither horse left the sort of print he was looking for.

That didn't have to mean anything, he told himself. The bushwhackers could still be Malone's men. They might be in the saloon at that very minute. They could have spotted him and sent Breck and Early out to kill him under the guise of a brawl that got out of hand.

Or maybe Breck and Early really were just a couple of troublemaking oafs, as Sophia had called them. The Kid couldn't be sure. Either way, they might have killed him if the woman hadn't stepped in.

He smiled at her as he stepped onto the board-walk. "I'm much obliged to you for your help," he told her. "I think I could have handled those two, but it would have been quite a chore."

She lowered the Colt, gave him a scornful look, and snorted. "A skinny hombre like you? They would have busted you to pieces, mister."

The Kid suppressed a surge of irritation. "Can I buy you a drink to show my gratitude?"

She turned toward the batwings, saying, "You don't have to buy me a drink. I own the place."

"Then I'll buy one for the house and increase your profits."

That offer made her pause and look back over her shoulder at him. "I never refuse to take cash from a paying customer. Come on in, Mister . . . ?"

"Morgan," he supplied.

Sophia pushed the batwings aside and called to one of the three bartenders behind the hardwood, "Drinks all around, Fergus, on Mr. Morgan here!"

A cheer went up from the saloon's patrons, many of whom had crowded up to the front windows to watch the fight. The three bartenders began to set up drinks for the house.

Sophia walked along the bar, pausing to shove the Colt Navy into the empty holster of a man standing there. "Thanks for the loan of the hogleg, Dandy," she told him.

He snatched his shapeless old hat off and said, "You're mighty welcome, Miss Sophia. Would you really have shot them fellas if they didn't do like you told them?"

Sophia smiled. "What do you think?"

Dandy gulped nervously. "I think I would've done just exactly what you said, ma'am!"

That brought laughter from the men around him. Sophia looked back at The Kid again and coolly crooked a finger for him to follow her. He glanced around the saloon as he did so. The Rattler's Den looked like a profitable establishment. A long, gleaming hardwood bar with a huge mirror behind it, busy poker games and a spinning roulette wheel, tables crowded with drinkers, crystal chandeliers . . . The place had success written all over it, and in the rugged frontier community, it was hard to believe that a woman owned it, and such a young and attractive woman to boot.

The Kid followed Sophia through a door at the end of the bar. It opened into a short hallway with several more doors. She swung one of them back and revealed a comfortably furnished office with a big desk and chairs upholstered in red Moroccan leather behind and in front of it. She closed the door and motioned for The Kid to take a seat in front of the desk while she went behind it.

"Do you invite all your customers back here to your private office?" The Kid asked as he sank into the leather chair and casually cocked his right ankle on his left knee.

"Only the ones I find interesting," Sophia said. She leaned back in her chair and swiveled it slightly from side to side. "You don't look like the sort of saddle tramp or grub line rider who usually drifts into Bristol, Mr. Morgan."

"You don't look like most of the saloon owners I've run into, either," he said. "They tend to have jowls, muttonchop whiskers, and big red noses."

Amusement danced in her astonishing green eyes. She had a tiny beauty mark just to the left of her mouth. At first glance, The Kid had taken her to be very young. He would have said that she was barely out of her teens. Now he saw that she was somewhat older than that, twenty-five or twenty-six, maybe. That was still awfully young for her to be running a saloon.

"What are you doing here?" she asked.

"I could ask the same thing of you."

She laughed. "Isn't it obvious? Making money hand over fist, that's what I'm doing."

"I just meant that it's unusual to find a woman—"

She held up a hand to stop him. "Don't start on that. You're probably like everybody else. You think I ought to find myself a man, settle down, and start popping out babies. Well, that's not going to happen." Her husky voice hardened. "Ever."

The Kid shrugged. "That's none of my business. I was just commenting on the fact that there aren't many saloonkeepers like you."

"You were avoiding my question, that's what you were doing. What brings you to Bristol?"

"Just passing through," The Kid said.

"And if I said I don't believe you?"

"I'd say it's not considered polite to call a man a liar," The Kid pointed out. "A woman in the saloon business probably ought to know that."

She appeared to be annoyed. The Kid figured that with her good looks, she was accustomed to having men falling all over themselves to give her anything she wanted. The fact that he seemed immune to her charms—even though he was well aware of them—probably bothered her.

"That gun on your hip," she said abruptly. "Are you any good with it?"

"Good enough to have stayed alive this long."

"What would you have done if Breck and Early had slapped leather instead of starting that rough-and-tumble? Could you have killed them both?"

"I don't reckon we'll ever know, will we?"

He could tell that she was getting more put out with him by the minute. What was the purpose of all these questions, he wondered. Was it possible that she had taken him for a professional gunman and wanted to hire him, like Diana Starbird had tried to do?

The answer to that question would have to wait. The door behind The Kid opened, and instinct brought him out of the chair as a man said, "Sophia, I wanted to—"

The newcomer stopped short, his eyes widening in surprise and alarm as he found himself staring down the barrel of The Kid's Colt.

Chapter 14

"Mr. Morgan!" Sophia said from behind the desk. "Don't shoot! He's a friend."

The man who had come into Sophia's office ventured an uncertain smile as he said, "I'll echo that sentiment. Please don't shoot me."

The Kid lowered the gun and took his finger off the trigger. "Sorry," he muttered. "Habit."

"A rather dangerous one for those who find themselves around you, I'd say."

The Kid holstered his gun and narrowed his eyes. "Most people don't sneak up behind me more than once," he said.

"Jefferson didn't sneak up on you," Sophia said. "He came into *my* office to see *me*. And while it would be preferable if he knocked in the future"—she gave the newcomer a look—"he didn't do anything wrong."

"Sorry, Sophia, about not knocking," the man said. He wore spectacles, and they had slipped down a little on his nose. He put a finger on them and pushed them up again. "It's just that I heard people talking about how you were out in the street waving a gun around a short time ago, and I wanted to make sure you were all right."

"I'm fine. A couple of Malone's hard cases were making nuisances of themselves again and brawling with Mr. Morgan here. I sent them packing."

A look of dislike came over the man's face at the mention of Malone's name. "I see," he said.

"Mr. Morgan, this is Jefferson Parnell. Jefferson, Mr. Morgan. I'm afraid I don't know his first name."

Parnell extended his hand. "I'm pleased to meet you, Mr. Morgan . . . especially since you're not pointing that gun at me anymore."

The Kid noticed dark stains on Parnell's fingers. "You're a newspaperman, are you?"

Parnell looked surprised. "That's right," he said. "How did you know I'm . . . Oh. The ink stains." He grinned. "Occupational hazard."

The Kid shook hands with him. Parnell had a strong grip. He was a big man, a couple of inches taller than The Kid and broad across the shoulders. His dark hair was rumpled, and several strands fell across his forehead. He pushed them back with his left hand, and The Kid got the impression that was sort of a nervous habit with the man, like pushing his glasses back up his nose.

Parnell didn't look like a journalist. As big and strong as he was, he looked more like he ought to be swinging a pick in a mine or wrestling a load of freight onto a wagon.

The Kid knew you couldn't judge a man by appearances, though. Some of the deadliest gunmen in the West were small and mild-looking, more like clerks than killers. He himself didn't look like a former business tycoon who was still a very rich man.

"If you were mixed up in that trouble, maybe I could get an interview with you, Mr. Morgan," Parnell went on.

The Kid shook his head. "I'm not interested in being in the paper. Sorry."

"Mr. Morgan's just passing through," Sophia said. "At least, that's what he claims." She pulled the purple plume out of her hair and toyed with it. "Personally, I think he's another hired gun that Malone has imported."

The Kid looked around at her with a frown. "I thought you said those men I had trouble with, Breck and Early, work for Malone."

"They do," Sophia said. "But you just got into town. You didn't know them, and they didn't know you. All of Malone's men are sons of bitches. Trouble follows them around." She smiled. "Is that an accurate description of you, Mr. Morgan?"

Unfortunately, it was, The Kid thought, but not for the reasons she meant.

"I'm not a hired gun."

"Judging by what I saw a few minutes ago, you're

fast enough on the draw to be one," Jefferson Parnell said.

"That doesn't mean anything."

Parnell's broad shoulders rose and fell in a shrug. "If you say so."

"Who's this fellow Malone you keep talking about, anyway?" The Kid thought he might as well try to get any information they might have.

Parnell perched a hip on the corner of the desk and reached into his coat to bring out a pipe. He didn't fill it or light it, just fiddled with it in his long, ink-stained fingers. "Terence Malone," he said. "He has a ranch near here."

"But that's not all he is," Sophia said. "Or all he used to be, I should say. He was a pirate. Black Terence Malone, they called him in those days."

"A pirate?" The Kid repeated, trying to sound as if he didn't already know all of this. "You mean like from a storybook? The Jolly Roger and the bounding main, all that?"

Parnell said, "There was nothing fanciful about his career, Mr. Morgan. He and his crew of brigands looted and sunk a number of ships in the Caribbean. Malone was a very dangerous man . . . and he still is."

"How do you know about this?"

"From another rancher named Owen Starbird," Parnell explained. "Starbird is a former British naval officer who hunted Malone down and put him in prison."

"Then what's Malone doing here in Rattlesnake Valley?"

"He served his sentence and was released," Parnell said.

The Kid nodded as if he had just figured out something. "And he came here to settle his old score with this fella Starbird."

"According to Starbird, that's the case. Malone tells a different story."

"What does Malone say?" The Kid didn't figure he would put much credence in Malone's version of the situation in the valley, but he wanted to hear it anyway.

"He claims he just came to the valley to settle down and make a new life for himself. But if that were true, why would he bring some of his old pirate crew with him?"

The Kid made his voice sound dubious. "He brought more pirates with him?"

Parnell nodded solemnly. "That's right. He hired a number of gunmen, too. Hard cases like someone would hire to fight a range war. I'm sure that's why Miss Kincaid here thought you'd come to Rattlesnake Valley to work for Malone."

"So I look like a hard case," The Kid said dryly.

Sophia said, "You got that Colt out of its holster in a mighty big hurry. What are we supposed to think?"

"Just because a man knows how to use a gun doesn't mean it's for hire."

The young woman's lovely bare shoulders lifted

and fell as she said, "I meant no offense." She looked like she had made up her mind about something. As she rose to her feet, she went on, "You bought a drink for the house, Mr. Morgan. Why don't you let me buy one for you?"

"And then?" The Kid asked.

"And then you can go on about your business."

A faint smile tugged at The Kid's mouth. "You're kicking me out of your saloon?"

"Not at all. You're welcome to stay as long as you want. I just don't want to keep you from doing anything you want to do. You should come and go as you please. Do we understand each other?"

The Kid nodded slowly. "I think we do."

He stood up as well, and Jefferson Parnell straightened from his casual pose leaning against the desk. The Kid turned toward the door, then paused.

"Since it was two of Malone's men I had trouble with, maybe I'd better ask you if there are any more of his men out there who might be holding a grudge against me."

"Because of that ruckus with Breck and Early?" Sophia shook her head. "I don't know who might have come in while we've been back here talking, but I don't recall seeing any more of Malone's men in the saloon when the fight started."

That was interesting, but The Kid carefully kept his face expressionless. At first he'd been certain that Breck and Early were the ones who had bushwhacked him and his companions at the river. Then, when he had discovered that neither of their mounts had that nicked horseshoe, he had speculated that the actual bushwhackers had sent two more of Malone's men after him.

Now, based on what Sophia had just said, it began to appear as if the bushwhackers hadn't come to the Rattler's Den at all when they reached Bristol. They might be anywhere in the settlement, or they might not have ridden into town at all.

He was going to have to work on becoming a better tracker, The Kid told himself. Given the sort of life he led, he couldn't afford to have dangerous enemies slip away from him once he was on their trail.

Of course, he couldn't learn everything at once. He didn't have the sort of seasoning and experience that most frontiersmen did. So far he had been getting by on instinct and his natural ability with a gun. However, it took more than that to ride the lonely trails and survive. His father was living proof of that.

Those thoughts went through The Kid's mind as he nodded to Sophia and said, "Much obliged." He slid a hand in his pocket and brought out a double eagle. "Is this enough to cover that round of drinks I bought for the house?"

She nodded. He tossed the coin on the desk, where it bounced and clinked. Then he turned and left the office.

Parnell hurried after him. "Don't mind Sophia," the big newspaperman said. "She can be a little hard to get along with sometimes. It's because she has to put up such a tough front in order to make folks take her seriously. Not many women own businesses, you know, and certainly not saloons."

"I suppose that's true," The Kid allowed as he and Parnell went in to the main room of the Rattler's Den. "How'd she come by the place?"

Parnell shook his head. "I don't really know. I've only been in Bristol about six months myself, and even though Sophia and I have become friends, I don't really feel like I can ask her personal questions, if you know what I mean."

"I do," The Kid drawled. "She might bite your head off if you did."

He went to the long, hardwood bar and found an empty space. Parnell moved in beside him, and as one of the bartenders came over, the newspaperman said, "Miss Kincaid offered to buy Mr. Morgan here a drink, Fergus."

The stocky bartender frowned skeptically at them. "Is that so?" He glanced along the bar and his demeanor changed. From the corner of his eye, The Kid saw that Sophia had emerged from the office as well, and he knew she must have nodded to the bartender. The man put his hands on the bar and asked, "What'll you have, Mr. Morgan?"

"Beer's fine," The Kid said, "as long as it's cold."

"Coldest you'll find in this part of the country," Fergus declared. "Just one more reason the Rattler's Den is the best saloon this side of El Paso."

Considering the vast, empty stretches of West Texas where settlements were few and far between, that might not be such an impressive boast, The Kid thought.

The bartender drew the beer and set it in front of The Kid. Parnell ordered one, too. He seemed determined to make friendly conversation. The Kid suspected that Parnell was still angling for a story for his newspaper. If that was the case, he was going to be disappointed. As long as Parnell was being talkative, The Kid intended to get information, not give it.

"Tell me more about this so-called pirate Malone, and the man he came here to get revenge on," he suggested.

Parnell was glad to comply. For the next several minutes, as they sipped their beers, Parnell told the same story that The Kid had heard from Diana Starbird: how George Starbird had settled in Rattlesnake Valley, uncovered the springs that fed the river, and turned the place into an oasis in the middle of the West Texas badlands. The rest of the yarn spun out the same, with Owen Starbird immigrating to Texas from England, and Black Terence Malone evidently following with the desire for dark and bloody vengeance in his heart.

"If everybody knows about this, how can Malone get away with what he's been doing?" The Kid asked.

"A little matter of proof," Parnell replied. "The Starbird ranch, Diamondback, has lost some cattle to rustlers, and somebody has taken potshots at the ranch hands, but no one has ever actually seen Malone or his men doing such things."

"I'm surprised the people in these parts put up with that. Don't the citizens here in town care what's going on?"

Parnell grunted. "Even if they did care, they'd be too scared of Malone to do anything about it. You can't expect a bunch of shopkeepers and clerks to go up against pirates and gunfighters, Mr. Morgan. Anyway, the days of everyone in Bristol feeling beholden to the Starbird family are over. A lot of people have moved in since George Starbird died, so they never knew him. And from what I gather, his brother Owen was never popular. Folks thought he was odd, and pretty much a cold fish. George Starbird had a daughter, a wildcat named Diana. All the cowboys who rode for the spreads in the valley other than Diamondback tried to court her at one time or other, but she ran them all off." Parnell shook his head. "So you see, no one here in town or in the rest of the valley is going to risk his life trying to help the Starbirds. They figure that Owen Starbird and his niece are rich, so they can take care of themselves."

The Kid felt a surge of anger go through him. Diana had told him how the settlers had turned their back on the family of the man who'd made it possible for them to live there, and now Parnell had confirmed it. The injustice of the situation and the ingratitude of the settlers rankled The Kid.

Parnell took a long swallow of his beer, then

went on, "You know, there's one person in this town who might have the gumption to stand up to Terence Malone." He inclined his head toward the end of the bar, where Sophia stood talking to the bartender, Fergus. "That's her, right there."

Sophia sensed them looking at her. She turned her head and frowned at them, then left the bar and went back through the door that led to her office.

"So," Parnell continued, "do you think you're going to be around here for long, Mr. Morgan?"

"Like I told the lady," The Kid replied, "I'm just passing through."

He had a hunch that things had gone far past that, though. The icy feeling along his spine told him that he wouldn't be leaving Rattlesnake Valley until more blood had been spilled and the air was full of gunsmoke.

Chapter 15

The Kid left the Rattler's Den a short time later, frustrating Jefferson Parnell as the newspaperman kept trying to angle for an interview. He walked up and down the streets, studying the settlement. Bristol didn't have a telegraph office, and he figured the closest railroad line had to be at least thirty or forty miles away. The Kid spotted a stagecoach station and thought about how odd it was, in that modern day and age only a few years away from a brand-new century, that a stagecoach was the town's primary means of communication with the outside world. It would probably be years before a railroad spur and the telegraph came to Bristol, and the telephone lines that were springing up across the West might not ever reach that far.

Something stirred in the back of The Kid's mind. A canny investor could come in there, pick up some land, maybe start working to get a spur line and a telegraph office . . . There was money to be made in Rattlesnake Valley, that was certain. All it would take was a letter to his lawyers in San Francisco to start the wheels rolling.

Then he stiffened as he realized what he was doing. Conrad Browning was the one who thought like that, not Kid Morgan. Those days were far behind him, and he was never going back to them again. Maybe he hadn't left that life as far behind as he'd thought.

He came across the doctor's office on one of the streets. It was an adobe house that obviously served as the medico's living quarters as well as his office. A sign out front read DR. NEAL EGGARS, M.D.

The Kid was surprised when he looked through the front window and saw a man moving around inside. The doctor should have been out at Diamondback, tending to Deuce Robinson's wound. Of course, the man in the house might not be the doctor, but The Kid was puzzled enough to go up to the door and knock on it.

The man who jerked the door open a moment later wore a harried expression and had blood on his hands. He was in his forties, with graying hair. "What is it?" he snapped. "Are you sick or injured, sir?"

"Not particularly," The Kid said with a frown, although his ribs did still hurt a mite from the brawl earlier. "If you're the doctor, I just want to talk to you."

"Then if you don't have a medical emergency, I'm already tending to a wounded man," the doctor said as he turned away.

The Kid grabbed the door before the man could close it in his face. "You *are* Dr. Eggars?"

"That's right." The doctor didn't try to force the door closed. He turned away, adding over his shoulder, "Come in and wait if you want."

The Kid followed Eggars into a waiting room, then on down a hallway. The doctor didn't realize The Kid was right behind him until they were both in a small room with an examination table in it. A man lay on the table, stripped to the waist, with blood oozing slowly from an ugly bullet hole in his shoulder.

Eggars jerked his head toward The Kid and said, "You shouldn't be in here—"

"I know this man," The Kid interrupted. He had recognized the wounded man as soon as he stepped into the room. The man lying bleeding on the table was the cowboy called Orrie, who'd been sent to Bristol by Sam Rocklin to bring the doctor back to the ranch. "How badly is he hurt?"

Eggars turned back to his work, picking up a wet cloth from a basin of water and swabbing at the wound in Orrie's shoulder. "This is his only injury," he said without looking around at The Kid. "The bullet lodged against the bone. It must have been a ricochet because it seemed to have lost some of its force before it struck him.

I don't believe the bone is broken. Luckily, I was able to remove the bullet once we got back here, but of course, that started the wound bleeding again. I'll finish cleaning it out, bandage it, and we can hope for the best. The young man lost quite a bit of blood out on the trail where we were attacked. He's in a very weakened condition."

The Kid had already seen that Orrie was only partly conscious and didn't seem aware of what was going on around him. He thought the young cowboy probably stood a good chance of recovering, though, if he didn't come down with blood poisoning from the wound.

"The two of you didn't make it to Diamond-back?"

That brought a glance from Eggars. "You know where we were going?"

"I was out there last night when Deuce Robinson was wounded and Jim Woodley was killed," The Kid replied.

The doctor's voice was grim as he said, "This is a bad business. There was enough tension in the valley to start with. Now that a man's been killed, it'll only get worse."

"More work for you."

Eggars frowned. "More work for the undertaker, you mean." He pressed a pad of clean bandages over the wound in Orrie's shoulder and looked at The Kid. "Who are you, sir?"

"My name is Morgan."

"You're a friend of the Starbirds?"

"I never heard of them until yesterday," The Kid answered honestly. "From what I've seen since I rode into the valley, though, it looks like they could use some friends. And since I had a run-in with Terence Malone and his men myself . . ."

"The enemy of my enemy is my friend, huh?" the doctor said. "There's an old Chinese proverb to that effect. Do you intend to stay in Rattlesnake Valley permanently, Mr. Morgan?"

"Only if I'm buried here."

"Then it seems the wisest course of action for you would be to ride on and forget about the Starbirds and Terence Malone."

The Kid smiled. "Nobody ever accused me of being wise. Why don't you tell me what happened to you and Orrie?"

Eggars began winding bandages around the puncher's shoulder to hold the dressing in place. "We were about halfway to Diamondback when someone started shooting at us from some rocks on top of a little hill. Orrie tried to return the fire, but he was hit almost right away. I travel by horseback, not in a buggy like some doctors, so I was able to grab his reins when he dropped them and lead his horse. He managed to stay in the saddle as we galloped away from there as fast as we could. After we had gone half a mile or so, I stopped and put a temporary dressing on his wound to slow down the bleeding. Then we headed back here to town."

The Kid nodded. From what the doctor said, it sounded like Malone had thrown a cordon of gunmen around the Starbird ranch. Those hired killers weren't going to allow any help to get through to Diamondback. That meant Malone might be getting ready to launch another all-out attack on the ranch.

"There's still a wounded man out there who needs your help, Doctor," The Kid said. "More than one by now, in fact. I reckon I can get you through, if you're willing to risk it."

"You can get me there and back safely? You guarantee that?"

The Kid's mouth tightened. "You're in the business of life and death. You know there aren't any guarantees."

"Then I can't come with you," Eggars said. "It's too risky."

"I thought you doctors swore an oath."

Eggars glared at him. "We do. The saddle-maker's wife is going to have a baby any time now, and I'm afraid it's going to be a difficult birth. The little daughter of the teller at the bank is running a high fever. Those are just two of my patients, Mr. Morgan, and I'm the only physician in Bristol. In this whole part of the state, actually. I have a lot more people depending on me than just a few cowboys at Diamondback. I did swear an oath, and I'm honoring it by not getting my head shot off because of some stupid range war!"

The Kid couldn't argue with that logic, but he grated, "It's not just a range war. Malone is out for vengeance on Owen Starbird."

"That's none of my business," Eggars said. "I'll help anyone who shows up on my doorstep, but I'm not going to put my life in danger recklessly. I wouldn't have gone with Orrie in the first place if I'd known what I was getting into."

The Kid bit back the bitter response he could have made. As far as he could see, his only choices were to either accept the decision Eggars had made, or pull his Colt and force the doctor to accompany him at gunpoint. He knew he wasn't going to do that.

"All right, Doctor," he said. "Take care of Orrie."

"Of course. I'll do everything I can for him." The doctor paused. "Are you going back to Diamondback, Mr. Morgan?"

"I am."

"Then there is one thing I can do. I'll pack up some medical supplies you can take with you. I don't know what they have on hand out there, so if they're facing more trouble, it might be a good idea to be prepared."

The Kid nodded. "Thanks. I'll pay you."

"All right. That's probably a good idea . . . as a precaution."

The Kid knew what he meant. If Black Terence

Malone has his way, Owen Starbird might not be around in the future to settle any debts, and the same was true for everybody else at Diamondback, too.

The Kid left the doctor's house a few minutes later, carrying the bag of medicine, bandages, and other supplies Eggars had gathered from the cabinets in his office. He walked back to the Rattler's Den but didn't go in to the saloon. Instead he tied the bag onto his saddle and unwound the buckskin's reins from the hitch rail. He was about to lead the horse over to a nearby water trough so that it could get a drink before he rode out, when Sophia Kincaid pushed the batwings aside and stepped onto the porch.

"Leaving town so soon, Mr. Morgan?" she asked.

"I think I've seen enough of Bristol," he said, not bothering to keep the tone of dislike out of his voice.

"I'm sorry we've disappointed you."

The Kid shook his head. "Not you. But I can't say I'm all that impressed by most of the other folks around here."

"You don't even know the people who live here. You don't have any right to say something like that."

"I know that nobody's got to the guts to stand up to Malone, except maybe you. Is that why you wanted to know if I was a hired gun? You want to pay me to go up against Malone?"

She came to the edge of the porch. "Say that Malone succeeds in destroying Owen Starbird. Do you think he's going to be satisfied with that? He'll wind up running this whole valley, including the town."

"And you're afraid he'll crowd you out," The Kid guessed.

Sophia's chin lifted defiantly. "I made this saloon a success. I won't have some bloody-handed pirate coming in and forcing me to take him on as a partner."

"You think that's what Malone's got in mind?"

"I know it is," she said. "He's already dropped some hints about how I need a man around to help me run the place." She gave a snort of derisive laughter. "As if I ever *needed* a man for anything."

"Seems to me you were just doing some hinting of your own, about me helping you," The Kid pointed out dryly.

Sophia shook her head. "I might be interested in hiring you, Mr. Morgan. But you'd be working for me. We wouldn't be partners."

"No thanks."

"You don't want to work for a woman?"

"I don't want to work for anybody at all. I'm just passing through, remember?"

"All right, then," she snapped. "Go on and leave.

When the time comes, I'll fight Malone by myself if I have to."

"Good luck," The Kid said. He lifted the buckskin's reins and led the horse toward the water trough, not looking back toward Sophia as he went.

Even though he had turned down her offer of a job, she wouldn't be fighting Malone by herself, he thought. With any luck, it would never come to that, because he intended to put a stop to Black Terence's reign of terror before Malone could take over the entire valley.

He just hadn't quite figured out how to do that yet.

Chapter 16

The Kid followed the main road west out of town. He felt eyes watching him as he rode out, and he remembered what Diana had said about Malone having spies in Bristol. He didn't doubt it for a second. As Malone gained more power in the valley, there would be more and more people in the settlement who were eager to curry favor with him. The Kid figured that before the day was over, somebody would be riding out to the Trident ranch to tell Malone everything that had happened in town.

Of course, Malone probably knew some of it already. He would have heard how Breck and Early had clashed with The Kid, and they might even have told him how Sophia had run them out of town, although it was possible they would balk at admitting that they had backed down to a woman.

As soon as The Kid was out of sight of the settlement, he veered the buckskin off the trail and set out across country. Malone didn't have enough men to cover every possible approach to Diamondback. The Kid intended to find a way through the ring of gun-wolves that Malone had thrown around the ranch.

He rode north until he came to the Severn River. That didn't take long, since the river and the main trail paralleled each other through the valley, the distance between them ranging from a half mile to a mile. The Kid reined in and studied the stream for a moment, trying to decide if it would be a good place to cross.

The Severn had a decent current in those places where the banks were fairly close together, telling The Kid that the springs in the mountains back to the west pumped out quite a bit of water. He turned his head to gaze toward the eastern end of the valley. Something tickled in the back of his mind.

He put the thought away since he couldn't quite grasp it and moved the buckskin forward. It was more likely that Malone would have men watching all the fords, he thought, so he would cross there. He wasn't sure how deep the river was, but the buckskin was a strong swimmer.

A few moments later, the horse emerged dripping from the stream and shook itself. The Kid continued to ride north for another mile or so, then turned west. The terrain was more rugged than it was around the headquarters of Diamondback, but there was still enough graze for the cattle he saw here and there.

All The Kid's senses were keenly alert as he rode. He knew that he might run into Malone's men at any time. He pulled the Winchester from its sheath and rode with it across the saddle in front of him, ready to use it if he encountered any trouble. His eyes constantly roved over the surrounding landscape, searching for dust that would mean riders or the glint of sunlight on metal that could indicate a hidden gunman drawing a bead on him.

In the end, though, it was his ears that told him something was wrong. He pulled the buckskin to a stop as he heard the sudden popping of gunshots.

The reports came from somewhere in front of him, and he guessed the distance at less than a mile. That was too close for the sounds to be coming from another attack on the ranch head-quarters. He was on Diamondback range now, though, so he figured Malone was to blame for the ruckus, wherever it was.

The Kid heeled the buckskin into a run. He galloped hard for several minutes, then pulled the horse back to a walk. He didn't want to charge right into the middle of a battle without knowing what was going on. The shots sounded a lot closer, so after a minute more, The Kid brought the buckskin to a stop and swung down from the saddle.

He dropped the reins, knowing that his mount would stay ground hitched, and started up a wooded hill. His hands were wrapped tightly around the Winchester.

Gunfire still rolled out like thunder somewhere

nearby. The Kid could tell that he was getting closer to it. He reached the top of the hill and saw that it was actually a long ridge that dropped down to a grassy flat on the other side. At the foot of the ridge, on the edge of the pastureland, stood a crude cabin with three walls built of mud-chinked logs and the fourth of stone. The cabin didn't appear to have any windows, but The Kid saw several rifle barrels sticking out through gaps between the logs on the side that faced the ridge. Flame spurted from the muzzles of the weapons as the men inside the cabin fired toward the ridge.

They had good reason for those shots, The Kid saw. Gunmen were scattered behind the boulders and trees that dotted the slope. They poured a concentrated barrage of lead at the cabin.

A horse whinnied shrilly somewhere close by. The Kid put a tree between himself and the sound and pressed his back against the trunk. It figured that the bushwhackers had left their mounts out of the line of fire, with a man or two to hold them. He didn't want to be spotted, so he took his hat off and edged his head carefully around the trunk for a look.

The horses were in a clearing about twenty yards to his right, below the crest of the ridge so that no stray bullets could find them. The Kid peered through the gaps between the trees and saw the animals moving around restlessly. Most horses, even ones used to gunfire, would probably get a little spooked by the continuing racket and the reek of burned powder in the air.

That meant the man responsible for holding them probably had his hands full keeping the horses calm enough so they wouldn't bolt. He wouldn't be expecting anybody to come up behind him.

The Kid darted through the timber, working his way toward the horses. For him, to conceive of a plan was to act on it. Caution had its place, but being hesitant could be deadly on the frontier. The trick, as Frank Morgan had explained to him, was to move fast but not be too reckless.

The Kid had no doubt that the cabin under attack was a Diamondback line shack, which meant that the men inside it rode for Diana Starbird and her uncle. The attackers had to be Malone's men. He didn't know how long the defenders could hold out, but he intended to even the odds a little.

Circling through the trees, The Kid came up behind the horses. He paused to count them. Ten mounts, and two men holding them, not just one. That meant there were eight gunmen hidden on the ridge above the cabin.

The Kid went all the way around the horses to come in from the north. The men wore dusters and had their hats pulled low over their faces. A frown creased The Kid's forehead as he saw that they had their bandannas tied around the lower half of their faces so that the colorful cloths served as masks. He supposed they were worried about being recognized.

He remembered that Malone was trying to carry out his campaign of revenge against Owen Starbird without leaving behind any proof. The former pirate had spent years in prison. He didn't want to take a chance on ever going back.

The Kid used the horses themselves to conceal him. He stepped around the animals and came up to the closest of the two men before the hard case even knew he was there. When the man spotted The Kid, he let out a startled curse and dropped the reins to claw at the gun on his hip.

The Kid struck first, moving with eye-blurring swiftness as he slammed the rifle butt against the side of the man's head. The man fell like a rock. The Kid didn't know if the blow had just knocked him out cold or cracked his skull and killed him, and he didn't really care. He still had the other bushwhacker to deal with.

The second man had heard his companion's startled reaction. He didn't try to brush his duster aside and reach for a pistol. Instead, he grabbed a sheathed Winchester on one of the horses and yanked it free. It belonged to either him or his companion, since the rest of the men had taken their long guns with them.

The Kid snapped his Winchester to his shoulder and fired first. The slug drilled into the man's chest and threw him back against the horses he had been holding. His finger contracted involuntarily on the trigger, making a shot explode from the rifle, but the bullet tore off harmlessly through the trees.

The Kid leaped forward and smashed the rifle's

stock across the dying man's face, shattering his
jaw and knocking him to the ground. A man could
pull the trigger on a gun even when he was drawing his final breath, so The Kid had learned not to
leave anything to chance. He kicked the bushwhacker's rifle away, then spun toward the far side
of the ridge.

The gunmen had to have heard the shots and
would likely send someone to see what had happened. But by the time anybody could get there,
The Kid had put the second part of his hastily-
formed plan into action.

He snatched his hat off his head and slapped it
against a horse's rump as he yelled, "Hyaaah!" He
struck left and right with the hat and used the Winchester's barrel to swat another horse. The animals
were already spooked, and that was all it took to
make them panic. A couple of them bolted for the
top of the ridge, and the rest followed, galloping
wildly through the trees.

The Kid ran after them and was close enough
to see what happened when the horses burst out
of the timber. Sure enough, another dust-clad,
masked hombre had been coming his way, but the
man suddenly found himself right in front of ten
stampeding horses. He barely had time to yell in
fear and throw his arms up in a futile gesture
before one of the horses slammed into him and
knocked him off his feet. His scream was cut short
as thundering, steel-shod hoofs pounded over him,

turning him into a bloody, broken mess in a matter of seconds.

The horses scattered as they started down the slope. Some of the bushwhackers were foolish enough to act on impulse and jump out of cover to try to stop the runaways. The Kid saw a man's hat fly off as blood exploded from his bullet-cored head in a crimson spray. Bringing the Winchester up again, The Kid dispatched another gun-wolf with a slug through the body. Then return fire forced him to duck back into the trees. Bark flew from the trunks around him as lead chewed into them. The bullets that missed buzzed through the woods like angry hornets.

The surviving gunmen realized that the situation had swung abruptly against them. The Kid heard a man bellow, "Let's get the hell outta here!" Another man shouted, "Grab those horses!" Shots continued to ring out.

Morgan ventured a look and saw that three of the men had managed to latch on to mounts. They leaped into the saddles and galloped away. Another man lunged for a set of trailing reins and missed, then spun around crazily as several shots from the line shack ripped through him. He was as limp as a rag doll by the time he fell.

That left just one of the bushwhackers trying to grab a horse. Seeing that he couldn't do it, he suddenly threw his rifle to the ground and thrust his arms in the air above his head.

"Don't shoot!" he cried. "I give up! Damn it, don't shoot!"

The Kid held his fire, and so did the men in the cabin. But one of the fleeing bushwhackers jerked back on his horse's reins, hauling the animal around in a circle. The man reached under the long coat to his waist and came up with a long-barreled Remington.

The Kid saw what was about to happen, but before he could call out a warning, the Remington blasted. It was a good shot for that range. The bushwhacker who was trying to surrender grunted and staggered back a step. He turned in a slow circle, bringing the ugly black hole in his forehead into view. The bullet hadn't gone all the way through his head, but it had sure turned his brain to mush, The Kid thought as he watched the man's knees unhinge. The bushwhacker flopped forward on his face as the rest of his body caught up to the fact that he was dead.

The Kid lifted his rifle and threw a couple of shots after the fleeing men, but they darted into the trees and over the ridge and he was pretty sure he hadn't hit any of them. Considering the damage he and the defenders in the line shack had done to them, he didn't think there was much chance they would double back and attack again. He kept a watchful eye out, though, as he went to check on the man he had knocked out.

A grimace pulled at The Kid's mouth when he saw the blood that had oozed from the man's eyes and nose and mouth. He had busted the varmint's skull, all right. The bandanna mask had slipped down and the man's hat had fallen off, but The Kid didn't recognize the hard, beard-stubbled face. He didn't think he had ever seen the man before.

The same was true of the man he had shot. He wondered how many hired killers Malone had working for him. Of course, hard cases weren't in short supply in that part of the country. Malone could just recruit more men to replace the ones he'd lost.

The Kid went back down the hill to fetch the buckskin. He led the horse up the slope. The tang of gunsmoke and the sheared-copper scent of freshly spilled blood made the buckskin's nostrils flare, but the horse didn't try to pull away. Such things were all too commonplace around Kid Morgan.

The Kid slid the Winchester back in the saddle boot and emerged from the trees into the open above the line shack. He held his right hand in the air above his head, open palm out to show that he was a friend. Several cowboys carrying rifles came out of the cabin, and one of them waved him down the slope.

As The Kid approached, the man who had signaled to him called, "I reckon you're the fella who stampeded them horses?"

"That's right," The Kid said. He came up to the punchers and went on, "You ride for Diamondback?"

"Damn right we do. Say, you're the hombre who

rode in yesterday with Miss Diana! Kid Morgan, right?"

The Kid nodded. He recognized a couple of the men. They were among the ones Rocklin had left to keep an eye on the ranch when he and the others had left that morning to trail the men who'd raided Diamondback headquarters the night before.

The attack on the line shack was the second act of open warfare in less than twenty-four hours. Obviously, Malone had run out of patience and intended to escalate his quest for vengeance on Owen Starbird.

That made it even more important that he get back to the ranch house, The Kid thought as he glanced at the sky. It had been a long day, and a lot had happened. Nightfall was only an hour or so away.

The way hell had started to pop in Rattlesnake Valley, there was no telling what that night might bring.

Chapter 17

The Diamondback hands wanted to know what The Kid was doing and why he'd happened to come along when he did. He thought they were still slightly suspicious of him, despite the help he had given them, and he supposed he couldn't blame them for that. They had to be feeling that everyone in the valley was against them, and they probably weren't too far wrong.

The Kid explained how Orrie and Dr. Eggars had been forced by gunfire to turn back before they reached the ranch headquarters. That brought bitter, angry curses from some of the men.

"If Deuce dies, it'll be that damn Malone's fault!" one of them declared.

"What about Orrie?" asked another puncher. "How bad was he hit?"

"The doctor thinks he'll pull through," The Kid said. "He'll be laid up for a while, though."

"That's one more mark against Malone," the Diamondback cowhand vowed ominously.

The Kid was in complete agreement with that. He asked, "What were you fellas doing out here?"

"Just checking on the stock in the east pasture. That bunch of gunnies jumped us, and we barely made it to the line shack so we could fort up."

"Anybody hurt?"

The cowboy shook his head. "A couple of bullet burns, but nothing to speak of. You say you've got medical supplies on your horse?"

"That's right," The Kid said.

"We'd better make sure you get through to the house, then. Folks there are liable to need 'em."

The cow ponies the men had been riding had scattered when they reached the line shack, but the animals hadn't gone far. They were grazing on the far side of the pasture. It didn't take long to round them up. The whole group started toward Diamondback headquarters with The Kid riding in the middle of the punchers. Since they knew that country a lot better than he did, he trusted them to get him back to the ranch by the best route.

It took another hour to reach their destination, which meant that the sun was setting when they got there, but at least they hadn't run into any more trouble along the way. The two big yellow dogs bounded out to bark at them as they rode in. Diana heard the canine commotion and hurried onto the porch to greet them.

"Kid!" she said. "Thank God you're all right.

I was worried you might not come back from Bristol alive."

The Kid swung down from the saddle. Sam Rocklin came up from the bunkhouse and said, "Gimme your horse, Morgan. I'll see that it's tended to."

"Thanks," The Kid said as he passed over the reins. He untied the bag of medical supplies from the saddle. Rocklin gave the reins to one of the punchers and followed The Kid up the steps onto the porch.

"Orrie never came back with the doctor," Diana said tensely. "You didn't happen to see them in town, did you?"

"Matter of fact, I did. They started out here this morning but got ambushed along the way."

Diana gasped. "My God! Is Orrie all right? Was Dr. Eggars hurt?"

"Orrie's got a bullet hole in his shoulder," The Kid said. "The doctor wasn't hit. Malone may have told his men to be careful and not ventilate Eggars. He's the only sawbones in these parts, according to what he told me."

Diana nodded. "That's right. How bad is Orrie?"

"The doctor thinks he's got a good chance. Eggars was able to get the bullet out of Orrie's shoulder, and if he didn't lose too much blood, he should be all right."

"Thank the good Lord for that," Rocklin said. "Boy's got the makin's of a good hand, could happen, he lives long enough."

The Kid hefted the bag in his hand. "The doctor sent along some medical supplies. He said you might be able to use them."

Rocklin took the bag and promised, "We'll put 'em to good use. Much obliged, Morgan, to you and the doc both."

Diana said, "Maybe I should go into town and see Orrie—" She stopped as The Kid began to shake his head.

"We got shot at when we crossed the river this morning. Then Orrie and the doctor ran into trouble. And I just came from the line shack over in your east pasture, where the men I rode in with were forted up while some of Malone's men tried to kill them."

Diana looked sharply at the men who had come in with The Kid. "Is that true, Josh?"

"Yes'm, it is," the oldest of the hands replied. "A bunch of gun-hung gents jumped us. We barely made it to the line shack in time to save our bacon."

"Well, thank goodness for that, anyway," she murmured. "You're sure it was Malone's men? Uncle Owen's bound to ask me about that."

The cowhand called Josh rubbed his angular jaw and frowned. "I can't rightly say for sure who they were. There's about half a dozen bodies a-layin' out there as wolf bait, and I can't say as I recognized a one of 'em." He looked around at the other punchers. "How about you boys?"

A chorus of head shakes and negatives was the

answer. One of the men said, "I never saw any of those varmints before, but they was hard hombres, no doubt about that."

"You left their bodies out there?" Diana asked.

"Their horses ran off," The Kid explained, without mentioning that he was the one who had stampeded those animals. "We didn't have any way of toting them in."

Diana looked at Rocklin. "Sam, get the wagon and fetch those bodies so they can be buried properly. Even a hired gun should have a decent burial."

Rocklin looked uncomfortable as he replied, "Ma'am, I ain't arguin' that point with you—although it seems to me that coldblooded killers like that deserve whatever happens to 'em—but the plain and simple fact of the matter is, by the time we could get back out there with the wagon, it'd be plumb dark, and anyway, the wolves and other scavengers've probably been at the corpses by now. By mornin' they'll be gone for sure, so it might be best just to leave things the way they are."

Diana looked like she wanted to order him to do as she told him, but after a moment she sighed and nodded. "You're right, of course," she said. "I think this should be reported to the deputy, though."

"That won't do a bit of good," The Kid said. "If he's like the rest of the citizens in Bristol, he's either already in Malone's pocket or too scared to buck him."

Diana gave him a level stare. "So you're saying we have to go it alone."

"Not completely," The Kid said. "I'm on your side."

"And I appreciate that. I'm sure my uncle does, too. But Malone will just keep bringing in more gunmen until he controls the entire valley. We'll fight him, of course, but the odds against us will be mighty high."

The Kid smiled. "Malone's got himself a small army. You just need one, too."

"That's right, but where are we going to get it?"

The Kid didn't have an answer to that question yet, but things were stirring around in his brain.

Before any of them could form into a coherent picture, he heard the thumping of Owen Starbird's crutches inside the house. The sounds came closer until the former naval officer loomed in the doorway.

"What's going on out there?" Starbird boomed. "Blast it, come inside where I can hear what you're saying. Morgan, is that you?"

"That's right, Captain."

Starbird balanced on his crutches and used one hand to swing the screen door open. "Come in. We were about to sit down for supper." He turned his head and called over his shoulder. "Carmelita! Mr. Morgan will be joining us!"

Diana put a hand on The Kid's arm. "Yes, come in. We want to hear about everything that happened in town."

The four of them went inside. Carmelita had already set another place at the table. Over the next half hour, as they made a meal off a pot of Carmelita's excellent tortilla soup with savory chunks of *cabrito* floating in it, The Kid told Starbird, Diana, and Rocklin about what he had found in Bristol, starting with the fight involving Breck and Early.

"Those two are bad hombres," Rocklin said with a frown. "They would've killed you if they'd got the chance, sure as anything."

"I reckon they would have tried, but thanks to Miss Kincaid, they didn't get that chance."

"Miss Kincaid," Diana repeated. "You mean that . . . saloon woman?"

The disapproval was plain in her voice. The Kid nodded and said, "That's right, she owns the Rattler's Den."

"What does she have to do with anything?"

"She borrowed a gun from one of her customers and made Malone's men back down before they could stomp me to death. I guess she didn't want my dead body littering up the street right in front of her place." The Kid smiled. "That would be bad for business."

"Did you talk to her?"

"Sure. I had to express my gratitude. I bought a round for the house, in fact."

"She's so . . . brazen," Diana said. "I don't like her."

That was pretty obvious, The Kid thought. He wasn't sure why Diana felt that way, unless it was a sort of natural jealousy that one attractive woman might feel toward another. There had been a time when he was confident that he understood women, but that was back when he was still young and stupid. Not even his father Frank understood women, despite being married a couple of times, and he didn't mind admitting it, either.

"Sophia's the only person I met in Bristol who seemed willing to stand up to Malone," The Kid pointed out. "She doesn't want him taking over the valley. Nobody else cares, as long as he leaves them alone."

Starbird said, "It's shameful the way people can simply turn their back on evil as long as it doesn't threaten them. I thought you American frontiersmen were supposed to have more of a sense of honor than that."

"Most do," The Kid said, "but I reckon times are changing. Even out here, a lot of people have lost whatever it was that made the pioneers special. They want life to be easy. They want somebody to hand them everything and take care of them." The Kid shook his head. "Malone has figured that out, and he'll take advantage of it as much as he can, for as long as he can."

Diana said, "But you're not that way, Kid. You'll still help us fight him."

The Kid shrugged. "Sometimes I'm just too stubborn for my own good." He went on to give them the details of his conversation with Sophia and Jefferson Parnell, then his visit to the doctor's house, and finally he explained about finding the battle going on at the line shack.

When The Kid was finished, Owen Starbird nodded and said solemnly, "Thank you for everything you've done on our behalf, Morgan. But despite what you said to my niece about helping us fight Malone, you simply can't."

The Kid frowned at Starbird in surprise. "Why not, Captain? That decision is up to me, isn't it?"

"This isn't your fight," Starbird replied with a shake of his head. "This land belongs to Diana and me. It was her father, my brother, who made this valley what it is. We're bound to it by blood. And it's the job of Mr. Rocklin and the rest of the men who work for us to defend it as well. It's their duty, although I wouldn't hold back any man who wished to ride away nor bear him any ill will for doing so. But you, sir . . . you won't take our wages, nor do you have any personal reason for declaring your opposition to that bloody pirate!"

"I've tussled with some of his men twice," The Kid pointed out, "not to mention been shot at a few times by men who were probably working for him."

"Is that enough reason to throw your life away?"

"Uncle Owen!" Diana exclaimed. "You're talking like we can't possibly win."

Starbird spread his hands. "What can we do? Malone has us surrounded. He's brought the hostilities out in the open. It's highly likely that he'll attack the ranch again, and even if he doesn't, he can cut off our supplies and starve us into submission while his rustlers continue stealing our stock. We don't have enough men to fight him, and the men we have are ranch hands not gunfighters."

Diana stared at him as if she couldn't believe what she was hearing. She said, "I never thought you'd give up. Of all the people I know, I figured you'd be the one to fight right until the bitter end, Uncle Owen."

"How can a man fight when he can't even walk? When you shoved me into that room and locked the door last night, Diana, you forced me to accept the truth at long last. I'm just a worthless old cripple."

"Aw, now, boss," Rocklin began, "don't talk like—"

"No, Sam," Starbird insisted. "It's the truth, I tell you. Diamondback is being run by a helpless cripple and a girl. What chance do the likes of us have against a ruthless pirate such as Malone?"

Diana came to her feet. "You didn't act like that when you were the captain of your own ship!" she cried. "You never give up. You captured Black Terence and sent him to prison!"

"Yes," Starbird said in a hollow voice, "and now we're all reaping the whirlwind for that, aren't we?"

The Kid leaned back in his chair and reached for the cup of coffee beside his empty soup bowl. "Captain," he said, "I know things look pretty bad right now, but Diana's right. You can't give up. Maybe it's true that your troubles aren't really any of my business, but I was brought up not to turn my back on folks who need help."

That was true in a way. The time he had spent with Frank Morgan over the past few years—and with Rebel—had taught him that. Those were the years when he had really grown up.

"I can't very well stop you, can I?" Starbird said. "All right, Morgan, you have my blessing—and my thanks—for whatever it is you can do to help us. I just hope it doesn't wind up getting you killed."

"That's a chance I'm willing to take," The Kid said.

Chapter 18

The Kid wouldn't have been surprised if there was more trouble during the night, but the hours of darkness passed quietly on Diamondback. The fevered state of his dreams wasn't so peaceful. Once again, all the men he had killed haunted him. He was still weary when he went down to breakfast early the next morning. He found Diana already in the kitchen with Carmelita.

"Have you been out to the bunkhouse to check on those wounded cowboys?" he asked the older woman.

"Sí," Carmelita replied. "I think Señor Deuce is better this morning, and the other two are not hurt too badly. Junior's wound looked worse than it really was."

"I agree," Diana said from her seat at the table. "I looked in on them, too."

"I'm sure they appreciated that," The Kid said as he took the cup of coffee Carmelita offered him.

Diana frowned. "What do you mean by that?"

"I never saw a man yet who didn't enjoy being fussed over by a pretty girl, especially a young cowboy."

"I didn't fuss over them. Anyway, I'm not a pretty girl to the hands, I'm one of their bosses."

"Hmmph," Carmelita said.

"Wait a minute." Diana put her hands flat on the table. "Are you telling me that some of those ranch hands are . . . are sweet on me?"

"They are young men," Carmelita said. "How could they not be?"

"Anyway," The Kid added with a grin, "I've been told that all the hands from all the other ranches in the valley have come courting at one time or another, before Malone got here, of course. You must know how popular you are with the cowboys, Diana."

"I know I'm not looking for a husband," she snapped. "Especially not some forty-a-month-and-found cowpoke who's just as interested in marrying a ranch like this as he is in me! And who in blazes has been telling stories about me? I'll bet it was that saloon hussy, Sophia Kincaid!"

"As a matter of fact, it was the newspaperman, Parnell."

"Oh." Diana frowned. "Well, he shouldn't be gossiping about me, and I intend to tell him as much the next time I see him. Anyway, there's no truth to it. A few of the cowboys in the valley may have tried to court me, but not all of them. Not hardly."

"Whatever you say," The Kid said. "Carmelita, you think you could whip up some *huevos rancheros*?"

"Of course, Señor Morgan."

The Kid turned back to Diana and asked, "Have you seen your uncle this morning?"

She sighed and shook her head. "I couldn't believe it last night when Uncle Owen said he was giving up. That's not like him at all. He was always a fighter, just like my father. I never knew him until he'd started having trouble with his legs, of course, but even then, he was eager to take any problem or danger head on."

"Man as proud as your uncle has a hard time relying on others for anything," The Kid said. "I reckon after a while the feeling just wore him down."

At the stove, Carmelita nodded. "Señor Morgan is right. Every man has his limits, señorita."

The Kid had come damn close to reaching his own limits when Rebel was killed. The tragedy had almost broken him. Even long months later, there were moments when he felt like she was still right there beside him, like he could reach out and touch the softness of her hair, smell the sweet scent of her, hear the caress of her voice. In those moments he still felt the sharp pain of losing her. Some of the wounded places inside his heart had healed, but others were still there and maybe always would be.

Anyway, he didn't want to forget her. That was the most frightening possibility of all. If the pain meant she was still with him in the only way she could be, then so be it. He could live with the pain. When the time came, he could die with it.

"Kid?"

The soft voice belonged to a woman, but it wasn't Rebel's. He knew that as he lifted his head and looked across the table at Diana Starbird. But he was shaken for a second, anyway.

"You suddenly looked like you were a million miles away, Kid," she went on. "Is something wrong?"

He forced a smile to his lips. "No," he lied. "I was just trying to figure out what to do about Malone. You know, if I rode up to his ranch, I don't think anybody could stop me from killing him."

"And you'd be dead a few seconds later! His men would fill you full of lead, Kid, and you know it. Trying something like that would be just plain suicide." Diana paused in her protest. "And it wouldn't stop the rest of that bunch, anyway. You think men like Wolfram and Greavy, or even Breck and Early, would just go away if something happened to Malone? If anything, he's been keeping them from ravaging the whole valley like a pack of wild dogs."

She was probably right about that, The Kid thought. He said, "All right, we'll think of something else."

Heavy footsteps clomped in the front room. Sam

Rocklin came in to the kitchen wearing a worried look on his face. Diana saw that and sat up straighter in her chair.

"What is it, Sam?"

"Maybe nothin', Miss Diana," Rocklin replied as he scratched at his jaw. "One of the fellas spotted some smoke west of here."

"A range fire?"

The Kid knew how dangerous and destructive such blazes could be. He didn't think it was likely that such a fire would spread in Rattlesnake Valley, though. All the grass was fairly green and wouldn't burn easily.

Rocklin shook his head. "No, it ain't that kind of smoke. Looks more like somebody's lighted a signal fire up in the mountains, not far from the pass."

That obviously meant something to Diana, judging by the sudden look of alarm on her face, and after a second The Kid figured out what it was as he remembered the errand she'd been on a couple of days earlier, when he met her for the first time.

"Gray Hawk!" she exclaimed.

"That's kinda what I was thinkin'," Rocklin said. "I've never been up to that old Injun's place, but you and your pa both told me about him. Seems like the smoke might be comin' from somewhere around there."

Diana was on her feet. "If he's sending smoke signals, something must be wrong. I have to go see about him."

"Hold on," The Kid said. "You know that Malone's men are lurking out there. If he's ready to declare all-out war on Diamondback, I reckon he'd love to get his hands on you. With you as a hostage, your uncle and the rest of the crew couldn't fight back."

"I know that," Diana said, "but I promised my father that I'd look after Gray Hawk. I gave him my word."

"You sure can't go up there by yourself," Rocklin said.

Diana frowned at him. "This is still my ranch, Sam. Half of it, anyway. Nobody tells me where to ride."

"What Sam meant is that you can't go up there by *yourself*," The Kid said as he stood up. "I'm coming with you."

"But Señor Morgan," Carmelita protested, "you have not eaten."

"It'll have to wait. Sorry."

Carmelita muttered something in Spanish. Rocklin sighed and said, "I'm comin' along, too, ma'am, and I'll get some of the boys to ride with us, if you're bound and determined to go up there."

Stubbornly, Diana shook her head. "No, Gray Hawk doesn't want a lot of people around. He doesn't trust anyone except me, just like he never really trusted anyone except my father. If a big bunch rides up there, it'll just spook him. He's liable to hide in the mountains where we'll never find him."

"If he's in trouble, seems like he'd want all the help he can get," Rocklin argued.

"I know, but I can't risk it." Diana looked at The Kid. "You can come along. I don't think it'll frighten the old man too much if he sees that there's just one other person with me."

"All right," The Kid said with a nod. "Let's go."

They hurried out of the kitchen with Carmelita exhorting them to be careful. Rocklin said, "You two go get your guns. I'll tell the boys to throw saddles on your hosses."

The Kid stepped onto the front porch a few minutes later, carrying his Winchester and Sharps. He turned to peer off toward the west, where the mountains closed off that end of the valley except for the narrow pass. A frown creased his forehead as something he couldn't put his finger on started to bother him, but before he could figure out what it was, Diana emerged from the house, the screen door banging behind her as she came onto the porch.

The Kid lifted a hand and pointed at a narrow, broken column of white smoke. "Yeah, it's there, all right, and it looks like it's coming from a signal fire, just like Sam said. See the way there are separate puffs of smoke?"

"I know what smoke signals look like," Diana said. "I'm certain they're coming from the vicinity of Gray Hawk's cave, too."

"He lives in a cave?" The Kid asked.

"He's a simple man. He doesn't need much, or want much. Come on, Kid."

Rocklin came out of the barn leading The Kid's buckskin and Diana's chestnut. They went down the porch steps and hurried to meet the foreman. Rocklin handed over the reins.

"I still say you ought to take some of us with you, Miss Diana," he urged.

She shook her head. "That would be a mistake, Sam. Trust me on this."

Rocklin nodded wearily. "Reckon I ain't got no choice but to do that."

The Kid and Diana mounted up and rode out, leaving Rocklin staring worriedly after them.

The sun hadn't been up long. Reddish-gold light washed over the valley, rolling in waves like the sea until it came crashing up against the mountains to paint the rugged, rocky slopes with brilliant colors. It was a beautiful scene, The Kid thought, but sometimes death and ugliness lurked in the midst of beauty. The truth of that musing was brought home to him by the sight of a diamond-back rattler squirming across the trail in front of them.

Serpents in paradise, The Kid told himself as he and Diana reined in to keep their mounts from shying at the snake. Wasn't that always the way?

Diana had belted on a handgun, in addition to bringing her carbine. She said, "Ugh," and reached for the revolver as she saw the snake, but The Kid stopped her from drawing the gun.

"Better leave it alone," he advised.

"My father taught me to shoot those scaly bastards every time I saw one of them."

"I don't doubt it, but if there's trouble up at the pass, a shot might warn whoever's causing it that we're on our way."

"That's true, I suppose. We'll wait and let it get out of the trail. Still, I hate to let one of them go." She shook her head and laughed hollowly. "Not that it ever did any good to kill them. They're still all over the blasted valley. I don't think anybody could ever wipe them out."

It only took a moment for the rattlesnake to slither across the trail and disappear into the brush. The Kid and Diana heeled their horses into motion and rode on toward the mountains.

"You say this fella Gray Hawk is a Yaqui?" The Kid asked.

"That's right."

"I thought Yaquis didn't get along well with whites . . . or anybody else, for that matter."

"Oh, yes, there was a time when they were fierce, according to what my father told me. Everyone in West Texas lived in fear of them. But then the Comanches pushed the Apaches farther west, and the Apaches pushed out the Yaquis. Most of them went south across the border to live in the mountains in Mexico. There were always some of them down there. Then the army drove the Apaches across the border, too. The Apaches still raid across the Rio Grande every now and then, but there haven't been any Yaquis around here for years, except for Gray Hawk. He's something of a rarity. In his younger days, he traveled widely, all over the West, something the rest of his people never did. He was friendly with my father, and, well, I guess you could say that he tolerates me."

The trail started to rise as they reached the foothills. Above them, the white puffs of smoke continued to climb into the pale blue early morning sky.

The Kid suddenly reined in and motioned for Diana to do likewise. As she brought her horse to a halt alongside the buckskin, she asked, "What is it, Kid?"

"Listen," he said.

Diana gasped as she heard it, too. The flat reports that echoed against the mountains could be only one thing.

Gunshots.

Chapter 19

"No!" Diana cried. "Gray Hawk!"

"He's probably fine," The Kid said. "The smoke wouldn't come up in puffs like that unless somebody was doing it that way on purpose, so he has to still be alive."

More shots rattled out, shattering the early morning stillness.

"But we'd better get up there before something does happen to him," The Kid went on. "Can you lead the way to that cave of his?"

"You bet I can!"

Diana sent her horse leaping ahead into a gallop. The Kid was right behind her, his buckskin pulling even with her chestnut within a few strides.

They followed the main trail for another half mile, which brought them close to the spot where The Kid had found the skull and crossbones and met Diana. She veered onto a smaller path that wound upward through rugged, prickly pear-covered ridges. The sun was high enough that the brilliant colors splashed over the mountains had faded. The peaks were granite gray again, with greenish-black splotches where stands of hardy pines found purchase in the rocky soil.

The shots had gotten louder and Diana was on the verge of panic from worrying about the old Indian. She was cool under fire when facing danger that threatened her, but whenever someone she cared about was in jeopardy, she had a harder time controlling her emotions.

"Take it easy," The Kid told her. "We won't let anybody hurt the old man. Why would Malone go after him in the first place?"

"I don't know!" Diana said. "It doesn't make any sense. Gray Hawk isn't a threat to anybody. He just wants to live out his days in peace."

The Kid didn't doubt that, but somebody sure seemed to think the Yaqui was a threat. Judging from the sound of the shots, half a dozen or more men were throwing lead at him.

Assuming, of course, that Gray Hawk was the target of that gunfire, The Kid reminded himself. He and Diana didn't know for sure yet.

"Over there," she said suddenly, pointing to a cleft that cut through a ridge. "That'll bring us out below his cave."

The Kid reached over to grab her reins and pull her chestnut to a stop at the same time he halted the buckskin.

"What are you doing?" she demanded as her face flushed with anger.

"We don't want to go charging in there without knowing what's going on," he told her. "How far is it from here?"

"To Gray Hawk's cave? About half a mile, I'd say."

The Kid nodded. "We'll leave the horses here and go on foot through that ravine."

"That'll take longer."

"Yeah, but we won't ride right into a storm of bullets that way."

She couldn't dispute that logic, so after a second she nodded. "All right. But we need to hurry."

They dismounted. The Kid tied both horses to a scrubby mesquite tree and took his Winchester from its sheath. He left the Sharps, thinking that it was unlikely he would need it.

As they started through the cleft in the rock, The Kid motioned for Diana to stay behind him, and to his surprise, she actually did it. Sheer stone walls towered above them for seventy or eighty feet, close enough together that the sky was only a thin blue line. The passage twisted back and forth, and within moments they couldn't see where they had left the horses. Nor could they see what was in front of them more than a few yards at a time. The possibility of danger lurked around every bend, The Kid supposed, but he didn't allow that to slow him down.

He couldn't very well slow down anyway, not

with Diana right behind him, urging him on at every step.

Suddenly, The Kid heard a horse whinny somewhere not far ahead. He held out his free hand to stop Diana. Leaning close to her so that he could put his mouth near her ear, he asked, "What's the terrain like where this ravine comes out?"

"It opens into a flat stretch at the base of a slope. That slope runs up a couple of hundred feet to a cliff that rises straight above it. Gray Hawk's cave is in that cliff, right where it meets the slope."

"Is there any cover down in those flats?"

Diana nodded. "There are quite a few boulders and chunks of rock that have tumbled down from the cliff face over the years. Quite a few gunmen could hide behind them and fire up at the cave, if that's what you're thinking."

"That's exactly what I'm thinking," The Kid told her. "Is Gray Hawk armed?"

"He has a bow and arrow he uses for hunting antelope and mountain goats."

"That won't do him much good against a bunch of hard cases like Malone's bunch."

"And he has a Winchester," Diana went on. "He's an excellent shot with it, too."

The Kid smiled. "Well, that's something in our favor, anyway. Stay here while I scout ahead."

"I'd rather come with you."

"Then if I get in trouble, there won't be anybody to save my bacon."

She looked like she wanted to argue some more,

but after a second she nodded in agreement. "All right. But be careful."

The Kid left her there and stole ahead. He slipped around a couple of bends and couldn't see her any more when he glanced back. He hoped she would stay put, because he had a pretty good idea what he was going to find.

The sound of horses moving around and stomping their hoofs warned him. He flattened against the stone wall to his left and edged forward cautiously until he could peer around the next bend. He saw a man holding the reins of half a dozen horses. Just like at the line shack, The Kid had come up behind his enemies.

He recognized the man holding the horses. He had seen the hard case a few days earlier, when he'd first encountered Black Terence Malone not far from there. The horse-holder was one of Malone's hired guns.

The Kid could tell from the way the gloom had lessened that they weren't far from the end of the ravine. It was probably just around the next bend past the spot where the horses were being kept. Stampeding the animals wasn't going to work there like it had at the line shack. To see what the situation was he had to get past the horses.

Which meant he had to get past the gun-wolf hanging on to their reins.

The racket of the shots was louder than ever, and the way the blasts echoed through the ravine, bouncing back and forth on the stone walls, made it difficult to hear anything. The Kid was lucky that his keen ears had picked up the sound of the horses moving around and warned him. He relied on those echoes to cover up any small noises he made as he catfooted around the bend and approached Malone's man.

The hard case never knew he was there. The Kid struck without warning, slamming the butt of his rifle against the back of the man's head. He eased up a little at the last second, not wanting to kill the man unless he had to. The hard case let go of the reins and pitched forward, out cold when he hit the sandy floor of the ravine.

The Kid grabbed the fallen reins to keep the horses from bolting. He made soothing noises as he looked around for some place to tie the animals. He didn't want them stampeding out of the ravine and warning their owners that something was wrong.

The cleft was bare of vegetation. There wasn't even a scrawny little bush he could have used, so he found a rock about the size of a man's head, wound the reins around it, and set it on the ground so that it would hold the horses in place. Of course, they could pull loose without much trouble if they wanted to, but The Kid hoped they would stay calm enough—at least for a few minutes—not to do that.

He stole forward again and just as he thought, right around the next bend the ravine came to an end, widening out into that open ground Diana had told him about. The flats were only about fifty yards across, and on the other side of them the slope rose to the cliff and Gray Hawk's cave.

Clouds of powdersmoke hung over the narrow flats. The Kid stayed back as far as he could and still get a look along the base of the slope in both directions. He saw the boulders and slabs of rock that had tumbled down from the cliff. Five men were scattered around behind them, all firing at an upward angle toward the black mouth of the cave that was visible where the slope and the cliff face came together. From down there, they couldn't fire directly into the cave, but they could ricochet slugs off its roof and try to get the old Indian that way.

Gray Hawk was still alive, though. As The Kid watched, he saw several more puffs of white smoke rising from the top of the cliff. That told him there was a natural chimney running all the way from the top down to the cave where the signal fire was located. Air currents sucked the smoke out of the cave and up that chimney.

The smoke signals had done their job. They had brought help. It was up to The Kid to pull Gray Hawk out of the trap.

He thought one of the gunmen was Greavy. Wolfram was nowhere in sight, nor did The Kid see Malone. He guessed the remaining four men were some of the hard cases Malone had hired when he came to Rattlesnake Valley to get his revenge on Owen Starbird.

The Kid figured that since he'd be taking them by surprise, he could probably gun down two or three of them before they knew what was going on. But he couldn't hope to get all five of them before they returned his fire. There was no cover at the mouth of the ravine. He could pull back into it where they couldn't hit him, but he wouldn't have a shot at them from that spot, either.

That meant he couldn't take on all five at once. He had to whittle down the odds first. He leaned the Winchester against the rock wall and left it where it was. Then he stepped out of the ravine and dashed toward the closest of Malone's men.

The hired killer was on one knee behind a large slab of rock as he fired upward at the cave. The Kid approached from an angle rather than come at him directly from behind.

He made it to within a few yards before the gunman spotted him. The man twisted toward The Kid and tried to bring his rifle around, but before he could fire, The Kid launched into a diving tackle that sent him crashing into the man.

Both of them sprawled on the sandy ground. The Kid's left hand closed around the rifle barrel and wrenched it to the side so his opponent couldn't bring the weapon to bear on him. At the same time, The Kid hammered a punch into the man's jaw that rocked the hard case's head to the side. The man's muscles went limp as The Kid knelt atop him.

Moving quickly, The Kid rolled the stunned hard case onto his belly and used the man's own belt to lash his wrists together behind his back. The Kid jerked the bandanna from around the man's neck and crammed it into the man's mouth. That made a crude but effective gag that would keep the hard case from yelling as soon as his senses returned to him.

With that taken care of, The Kid knelt behind the slab of rock and studied the layout. About forty feet to his right, he saw another man standing behind a boulder. The Kid's view of the gunman was partially obstructed, which meant the man couldn't see him very well, either. The Kid took a chance and dashed toward the rock.

Flattening against the boulder, The Kid slid around it with his back pressed to the stone. He pulled his Colt from its holster, reversed his grip on it, and moved swiftly around the boulder until he could see his quarry. The man opened his mouth to let out a yell, but before any sound could escape, the butt of The Kid's revolver smashed down on his head.

The man's hat cushioned the blow a little, but not enough to keep the man from being driven to his knees. The Kid struck again, and the hard case toppled forward, out cold. Knowing that the man wouldn't regain consciousness for several minutes,

The Kid didn't take the time to tie him up. Instead he crouched next to the rock and tried to figure out how to best approach the third man. He had cut the odds down, but they were still three to one.

He didn't realize he'd been spotted until a voice suddenly called out, "Freeze, you son of a bitch!"

Chapter 20

The Kid glanced to his left and saw Greavy stepping out from behind another slab of rock with a rifle in his hands. The Winchester was trained on The Kid's head, and he knew it would take only the slightest pressure from Greavy's finger to send a bullet through his brain.

So he did the only thing he could. He froze.

Greavy came farther into the open. "Morgan!" the little gray-clad gunman spat. "I knew you were gonna be trouble. Black Terence should've let me go ahead and kill you after you beat Wolfram."

"You could've *tried*," The Kid said, letting his lip curl a little in contempt.

That resulted in the effect he wanted. Greavy said, "I've heard about you, you bastard. You're supposed to be fast."

"No supposed to be about it."

Greavy hesitated, but only for a second.

"Holster that gun!" he snapped. "Careful! I'll kill you in a heartbeat if you try anything funny."

The Kid lowered the Colt, shifted his grip on it, and slid it slowly into leather. Then even though Greavy had told him to freeze, he turned so that he faced the little gunman squarely.

"What now, Greavy?" he asked. "You're calling the tune."

"Damn right I am. We're gonna settle this, Morgan. We're gonna find out once and for all which of us is faster."

"You know," The Kid drawled in apparent unconcern, hammering in the final nail, "I haven't lost any sleep worrying about that."

"You're about to have a long sleep, Morgan. The longest sleep of all."

Before The Kid could respond to that, one of the other gunnies called, "Hey, Greavy! What the hell's goin' on? Why'd you and Hainsworth and Douglas stop shootin'?" The question didn't surprise The Kid, since he had noticed that all their guns had fallen silent.

"Hainsworth and Douglas are out cold!" Greavy shouted back. "And I've got the son of a bitch who done it!"

"What do you want us to do?" That question left no doubt that Greavy was in charge of the group of hard cases.

"Keep that old redskin pinned down! If he shows his face, blast it!"

The other man said, "I thought the boss told us not to kill him."

"Unless we had to!" Greavy said. "It's up to me!"

So Malone didn't particularly want Gray Hawk killed. That was an interesting bit of information, The Kid mused. Maybe if he lived through the next few minutes, he could figure out what it meant.

"I'm getting bored here, Greavy," he said. "If we're going to settle anything, let's get to it."

Greavy snarled, and for a second The Kid thought he had pushed the weasel-like gunman too far. Greavy looked like he was ready to shoot The Kid with the rifle and be done with it.

But then he lowered the Winchester. In fact, he set it aside, leaning the barrel against the rock beside him.

"All right," Greavy said as he straightened from doing that. "Count of three?"

"Fine by me," The Kid said.

"One," Greavy called, and as soon as the word was out of his mouth, his hand stabbed toward the gun on his hip.

The Kid was expecting just such a treacherous trick. As soon as he saw Greavy's hand start to move, he began his own draw. Greavy was fast, all right, mighty fast. His gun seemed to leap out of its holster and into his hand faster than the eye could follow. The barrel came up and leveled just as fast.

But Kid Morgan was faster. By the time Greavy

pulled the trigger, The Kid's Colt had already
blasted fire and lead from its muzzle. The slug
slammed into Greavy's chest just a shaved heartbeat before the little gunman's revolver roared.

That was enough to throw off Greavy's aim. The
Kid felt as much as heard the whipcrack of air as
Greavy's bullet rushed past his ear.

Greavy was still on his feet, although the impact
of The Kid's bullet had forced him to take a step
backward. His eyes widened with pain and surprise
and horror at the fact that he was dying. His mouth
opened but no sound came out as he struggled to
raise his gun and fire again.

The Kid shot him a second time. The bullet
bored into Greavy's forehead and smashed through
his brain, causing the back of his skull to explode
in a grisly crimson spray. Greavy fell, seeming to
fold in on himself like a house of cards collapsing.

Instinct warned The Kid to move. He spun to his
left just as a rifle cracked and a bullet whistled
through the space where his head had been a second
earlier. He spotted the man who had shot at him, and
as the hired gunman tried to work the lever on his
Winchester, The Kid sent a shot in his direction
that tore his throat out. The man dropped his rifle
and staggered to the side as blood spurted from his
ruined throat. He made a terrible gagging sound
and pawed at the hideous wound for a second
before falling limply to the ground.

That left just one of Malone's men unaccounted
for, and he couldn't reach his mount to flee. The

Kid was between him and the horses. The Kid ducked behind one of the boulders as a shot blasted and the bullet chipped granite slivers from the stone.

Suddenly, shots came from the mouth of the cave. Old Gray Hawk was taking a hand in the game. Diana had said that the Yaqui was good with a rifle. Gray Hawk proved it by peppering the rocks with lead where the remaining gunman had taken cover. Bullets ricocheted wildly. The Kid heard the hard case shout a curse, then the man stumbled into view as slugs kicked up dirt around his feet.

The Kid could have killed him then without any trouble, but instead he drilled the man's thigh. The gunman yelled in pain as he twisted around and fell. He tried to struggle back to his feet, but his wounded leg wouldn't support his weight. He had dropped his gun when he fell, and as he stretched out his arm to grab it again, The Kid put a bullet into the ground just in front of the man's reaching fingers.

"Try again and I'll stop wasting time," The Kid called. "I'll just go ahead and kill you."

The man pulled his arm back. "Don't shoot!" he said. "Don't shoot, mister. I'm done." His voice was husky and strained from the shock and pain of his wound.

The Kid thumbed fresh cartridges into the Colt. He smiled. His gun had been empty when he made that threat. He snapped the cylinder closed and stepped into the open, keeping the revolver trained on the fallen man as he approached.

"You gotta help me, Morgan," the hard case said with a groan. "I'm gonna bleed to death here."

The Kid kicked the man's gun well out of reach but didn't holster his own Colt. He looked at the man's leg and saw blood pumping steadily from the wound. The man really was in danger of bleeding to death.

"All right," he said. "I'll see what I can do. Give me your bandanna."

The man took off the neckerchief and handed it up to The Kid, who finally holstered his gun. Being careful not to get the Colt where the wounded hard case could reach it, he twisted the bandanna into a strip of cloth that he slid around the man's upper thigh. There were no sticks lying around, so he couldn't make a proper tourniquet, but he pulled the bandanna as tight as he could and tied it in place. Blood still flowed from the wound, but it slowed to a trickle.

"Th-thanks," the man gasped. He looked like he was on the verge of passing out from losing so much blood.

A second later the man's hand suddenly came up with a two-shot derringer cradled in it, clearly intending to take The Kid by surprise and kill him.

He had not reckoned with the amazing reflexes of Kid Morgan, however. The Kid palmed out his Colt and fired just as the little derringer gave a wicked pop. Those weren't the only shots to echo against the cliff face. The sharp crack of a rifle came from somewhere above The Kid. His own bullet ripped through the hard case's body. The slug from the rifle splattered the man's brains all over the sand. He wouldn't have to worry about bleeding to death. He was already shaking hands with the Devil.

The Kid turned his head to look up the slope toward the cliff. A tall, straight figure stood there with a rifle in his hands. The man wore denim trousers and a baggy white shirt. He had a blue sash tied around his waist, and a band of red cloth circled his head and held back long, iron-gray hair that blew in the wind.

That would be Gray Hawk, The Kid thought. The Yaqui started down the slope toward him, moving carefully so that his feet, shod in rope sandals, didn't slip on its gravelly surface.

As Gray Hawk reached the bottom of the slope, The Kid nodded to him and said, "Much obliged for the help." He didn't know how well the Yaqui understood English.

Evidently Gray Hawk understood just fine, because he returned the nod and said in a deep, powerful voice that age hadn't weakened, "I express the same sentiment, señor. You and I killed this dog at the same time, but you dispatched four of them before that."

"Actually, I just killed two of them," The Kid said. "The other two are still alive."

Gray Hawk held his Winchester at his side in his

left hand. At The Kid's words, his empty right hand stole toward the sash around his waist. The blade of the knife tucked behind the sash gleamed in the morning sun.

"I can deal with them," the Yaqui said. His voice was expressionless, but it was all the more grim because of that.

The Kid shook his head. "I want them alive. Miss Starbird and I will take them to Diamondback."

For the first time, The Kid saw some animation in the Indian's dark eyes and a slight softening in the coppery, hawklike features that had been seamed and weathered by time.

"The señorita is with you?" Gray Hawk asked. "I thought she might see my smoke."

The Kid nodded. "That's right. I left her back there in the ravine."

He half turned to gesture toward the mouth of the cleft in the ridge, then froze as he saw Diana being forced out by the man who'd been holding the horses. The hard case had his left arm looped tightly around her neck, and his right hand held a gun pressed to her head.

Chapter 21

Diana's mouth moved soundlessly. She couldn't say anything because of the arm pressed against her throat, but The Kid thought it looked like she was trying to curse.

He didn't doubt that for a second. He felt like cursing, too, and directing most of the angry words toward himself for leaving an enemy alive behind him, even an unconscious one.

But Diana came in for some of that anger. If she had stayed put, like he'd told her, she wouldn't have been where Malone's man could grab her.

She had grown impatient as well as worried, standing there listening to all the gunfire. No doubt she had wanted to see what was going on and make sure that The Kid and Gray Hawk were all right, especially when the guns fell silent. The Kid could imagine her creeping through the ravine, past the horses and the unconscious hard case, who hadn't really been unconscious at all as he got to his feet and slipped up behind her . . .

Such speculation was pointless, The Kid told himself. All that really mattered was that Diana was a prisoner, a hostage with a gun at her head.

"Drop 'em!" the man screeched at The Kid and Gray Hawk. "Drop those guns right now, or I'll kill her!"

"No, you won't," The Kid said. He forced his voice to sound calm. "You know as well as we do that if you pull that trigger, you'll be dead two seconds later. You won't have time to kill either of us before we put lead in you."

"We will not stop, either," Gray Hawk said. "We will continue firing until you are so full of holes *el Diablo* himself will not recognize you."

The hard case looked shaken by the threats, but he wasn't ready to back down just yet. "Maybe so," he said, "but the girl will still be dead."

"What is it you want?" The Kid asked.

"I told you." The man's voice trembled a little. "Drop your guns."

Slowly, The Kid shook his head. "That's not going to happen. You let go of Miss Starbird, and maybe we'll let you get on one of those horses and ride out of here with your whole hide."

The man looked tempted, but he didn't loosen his grip on Diana. "I know as soon as I let go of her, you'll shoot me," he said. "I can't risk it."

"Back up toward the ravine," The Kid suggested. "When you're far enough back that you can't see us and we can't see you, you can let go of her. That'll give you a chance to get mounted and make it around the first bend before we can come after you."

"Maybe . . . but you'll still come after me."

"No," The Kid promised. "We won't. Because I *want* you to go back to Black Terence and tell him what happened here. Tell him that whatever reason he had for trying to grab Gray Hawk, it failed. Tell him Greavy and those other men are dead, and that we have two more of his men prisoner."

"Greavy's dead?" the man repeated in an awed voice, as if he couldn't believe that anybody could kill the ugly little gunman. "You got the drop on him from behind?"

The Kid shook his head again. "Took him on straight up and beat him to the draw."

The gunman let out a startled whistle. "I didn't think anybody was faster'n Greavy."

"There's always somebody faster," The Kid said. "Now, are you going to take the deal? You know it's the only way you'll get out of here alive."

"Yeah . . . yeah, hold on, lemme think." The man started backing toward the ravine, taking Diana with him. "Don't shoot. I got your word, right?"

"My word," The Kid confirmed with a nod.

He saw Diana's eyes blazing with anger, and he knew she didn't like the fact that he was making a deal with one of Malone's men. She would rather have taken her chances in a shootout, The Kid supposed. But he wasn't going to risk her life needlessly, and besides, he really did want the gunman to carry that message back to Malone. The mocking words might provoke Malone into a rage that would make him do something stupid.

The gunman vanished from sight in the dark mouth of the ravine. Diana had no choice but to go with him. But a second later, she came back into view, stumbling forward as if the man had given her a hard shove. With a cry of mingled pain and fury, she fell to her knees.

The Kid leaped forward to run to her side. Gray Hawk was right behind him. By the time he and the Yaqui reached Diana, they could both hear the frantic pounding of hoofbeats as the hard case fled up the ravine.

"I hope you're happy with yourself!" Diana cried as she looked up at The Kid. "You let him get away!"

"One hired gunnie more or less doesn't make any difference," he said. "Malone's the one who matters, and he's not here."

Diana scrambled to her feet, pointedly ignoring the helping hand that The Kid extended toward her. She turned to the Yaqui and asked anxiously, "Gray Hawk, are you all right?"

"Sí, señorita. Those men thought to slip up on Gray Hawk and take him by surprise." A faint smile curved the old Indian's mouth. "They were foolish to believe that they could do such a thing."

"Very foolish indeed," Diana agreed. "I'm glad you holed up in your cave and sent signals to me, as we agreed you would do if you ever found yourself in trouble."

The Kid looked at her. "You didn't tell me you had a whole system worked out."

"I didn't think it was any of your business," she said. "You were coming with me to help Gray Hawk, and that was all I cared about."

The Kid turned his attention back to the Yaqui. "Do you have any idea why Malone would want to capture you?"

"None, señor. I have nothing to do with what goes on in the valley. All I want is to be left alone here in the mountains to live in peace."

The Kid frowned as he thought. "Malone knows how fond of you Diana is, though," he mused.

"What does that have to do with anything?" she asked.

"Malone might think that if he got his hands on Gray Hawk here, he could use him as leverage against you, to get you to do something Malone wants you to do."

Diana paled. "Like agree to marry him? And he'd threaten to kill Gray Hawk if I didn't?"

The Kid shrugged. "Could be. It's just a possibility. I don't know how Malone thinks."

"It's just the sort of evil thing he'd do," she declared.

Gray Hawk said, "Whatever this man wants with me, you need not worry, señorita. He will never take me alive."

"I know," Diana said, "because you're coming back to the ranch with us, Gray Hawk."

The Yaqui frowned and shook his head. "That is not the place for me. I belong here, in the mountains."

"Didn't you tell me that you traveled all over the West when you were younger and had all sorts of adventures?"

Gray Hawk inclined his head in acknowledgment of that point. "As you say, I was younger then. Now I am old and care not for traveling."

"It's only a few miles to Diamondback. And you'd be safe there."

"I am safe here."

"You can't be sure of that," Diana argued. "Malone may come after you with all his men. If you're alone, you might not be able to stop them. Come with us, so that I can know that you're safe."

"Better yet," The Kid said, "come with us so you can help us keep Malone from taking over the whole valley."

He thought that the possibility of getting in on the fight might appeal more to Gray Hawk's nature. Judging by the sudden flare of interest in the Yaqui's dark eyes, The Kid's hunch was right.

"I have battled against many evil men in my time . . ." Gray Hawk said.

"I don't doubt it. We can use your help."

Gray Hawk studied him intently. "Who are you, señor? I took you at first for one of the men who ride for the señorita and her uncle, but now I see that you are a different sort of man."

"They call me Kid Morgan. I'm not from around here, but I've thrown in with Miss Starbird and her uncle against Malone. I don't like pirates, and it looks like he hasn't changed any since the old days."

"Morgan," Gray Hawk repeated as his eyes widened slightly. "I once knew a man called Morgan. A good man, with a fast gun like yours."

The Kid wasn't surprised that Gray Hawk had run into his father sometime in the past. Frank Morgan had gotten around, traveling all over the West many times, and wherever trouble broke out, The Drifter usually wasn't far off.

He didn't want to explain all that to Gray Hawk and Diana, though, so he just said, "Maybe your old friend and I are related."

"Perhaps," Gray Hawk said. He drew in a deep breath. "All right. I will come to the ranch with you. But remember . . . you promised me another fight against this man Malone."

"You'll get it," The Kid said.

With Gray Hawk's help, The Kid tied up the other two men he had knocked out and hoisted them onto their horses, draping them over their saddles and lashing them in place. The men were starting to come around, and as their senses returned to them, they howled and cursed bitterly at the uncomfortable predicament in which they found themselves. The Kid ignored their complaints.

Despite Gray Hawk's obvious age, he was still vital and seemed to be as strong as a horse. Hints of the natural savagery of his people lurked in his eyes, too. He would make a good ally in the fight against Malone.

It might be time to take that fight *to* Malone, instead of waiting to see what he would come up with next. Some of the smaller ranchers in the valley had had their barns burned down to make them toe Malone's line, Diana had said. Malone wouldn't like it if *he* lost a barn or two.

Since they had the extra horses, they also loaded the bodies onto the animals. Diana had been upset that the men who'd attacked the line shack hadn't received a decent burial. It wouldn't cost much time and trouble to see that the three corpses got laid to rest properly, although to The Kid's way of thinking that was more consideration than they deserved, especially Greavy. The hands on the ranch could bury them, though.

Leading the horses, The Kid and Gray Hawk started toward Diamondback. Diana rode a short distance in front. The men were alert and kept an eye out for any signs of trouble, but they didn't run into more of Malone's gun-wolves or anything else that delayed them. It was still morning when they rode up to the ranch headquarters.

Diamondback had visitors, The Kid saw. A buggy was parked in front of the house.

"Who's that?" he called to Diana.

"I don't have any idea," she replied with a shake of her head as she turned in the saddle to look back at him. The screen door banged and she hipped around to the front again.

Two people stepped onto the porch. The Kid recognized the tall, broad-shouldered figure of Jefferson Parnell, the newspaperman from Bristol.

Standing beside Parnell, wearing a neat, bottle-green outfit with a plumed hat of the same shade, was the owner of the Rattler's Den, Sophia Kincaid.

Chapter 22

The Kid noticed how Diana stiffened in the saddle at the sight of Sophia. On the porch, Sophia's chin took on a defiant tilt as she returned Diana's glare. The two women didn't like each other, that was for sure.

With the thump of crutches, Owen Starbird appeared in the doorway. Parnell quickly opened the screen, saying, "Let me get that for you, sir."

"Thank you," Starbird said as he awkwardly came onto the porch. "Diana, are you all right? Rocklin told me how you went chasing off to the mountains because of some sort of . . . smoke signals."

"Gray Hawk was in trouble," Diana said. "I had to go help him. It's a good thing I did, because Malone's men were trying to capture him. If they failed at that, they were going to kill him if they could."

Starbird looked at the Yaqui and nodded. "Gray

Hawk. It's good to see you again. It's been a long time since you've been to the ranch."

"It is good to see you as well, señor."

Starbird gave a bark of bitter laughter. "There's nothing good about seeing me, old boy, unless you enjoy the sight of a pathetic cripple."

The retired naval officer might have gotten a raw deal, but The Kid was tired of listening to him feel sorry for himself, especially when so much trouble threatened the valley. He wondered, too, why Sophia and Parnell had come to Diamondback, so he asked them bluntly, "What are you two doing here?"

"It's my buggy," Sophia said, "and Jefferson and I want to talk to you. He overheard something in the saloon that he thought you ought to know about, and when he told me, I agreed with him." She made a face as she looked at the horses trailing behind The Kid and Gray Hawk, then she added hesitantly, "Are those . . . dead bodies on those horses?"

"Only some of them," The Kid drawled.

As if to prove his point, the two who were still alive began cursing and complaining again. Sam Rocklin and some of the punchers had come up to see what was going on, and Rocklin gave one of the prisoners a hard swat on the back of the head.

"Shut that filthy piehole, mister," the foreman said. "There's ladies present, if you didn't know it . . . which I'm bettin' you did." He looked up at Starbird. "What do you want us to do with these hombres, boss?"

Starbird deferred to The Kid. "Mr. Morgan? What do you suggest?"

"I'd make sure they were tied up good and tight and stash them in the smokehouse for now," The Kid said.

That suggestion brought a pleased grin to Rocklin's rugged face. "What about the ones who're buzzard bait?"

"Find an out-of-the-way place to bury them."

Rocklin nodded. "We'll take care of it." As he moved up alongside one of the corpses, he exclaimed, "Good Lord! Is that Greavy?"

"Yeah," The Kid said.

"You done for him?"

"He wanted to find out which one of us was faster."

"Reckon that was a mistake on his part, since it looks like you blowed the whole back of his head off." Rocklin waved some flies away from the gruesome mess.

The Kid saw both Diana and Sophia shudder at Rocklin's blunt statement. Starbird must have noticed, too, because he said, "Take them away, please, Sam. The live ones *and* the dead ones."

"You got it, boss." Rocklin motioned and his men took hold of the reins and led the horses toward the barn.

With those grisly companions gone, The Kid, Diana, and Gray Hawk swung down from their saddles. Ranch hands took their horses, including the Yaqui's pinto. As The Kid started up the steps, he said, "I want to hear more about what it was that brought you out here, Parnell."

"Let's go inside," Owen Starbird suggested. "The sun is starting to get rather warm. Sam, I want you to hear this, too."

Parnell held the door for him again, and Starbird clumped back inside, followed by the others. Diana and Sophia kept their distance as they eyed each other warily. Gray Hawk looked a little uncomfortable, and from the way the Yaqui kept glancing around, The Kid figured he wasn't used to being inside a house and didn't like it very much. The Diamondback ranch house was a far cry from a cave in the side of a mountain . . . but from the looks of it, Gray Hawk preferred the cave.

"Carmelita!" Starbird called to the servant. "We have guests for dinner."

Carmelita came out from the kitchen, looked around at the visitors, and seemed surprised to see Gray Hawk. But she just nodded, said, "Sí, señor," and left the room.

Starbird lowered himself into his wheelchair. "Please, Miss Kincaid, Mr. Parnell, sit down. You were about to tell me what you learned in town when my niece and her friends came up."

Sophia and Parnell took seats on one of the leather-covered divans. Diana sat in a chair as far away from Sophia as she could get. Sam settled comfortably across from her. Gray Hawk crossed his arms and stood stolidly near the fireplace. His stance bore a certain resemblance to a cigar-store Indian, The Kid thought.

As for The Kid, he took his hat off and put it on his knee as he sat down in a leather armchair where he could see both Diana and Sophia. If the two of them started a brawl, he didn't want to get in the middle of it, he told himself.

Sophia said, "You tell the story, Jefferson. You were the one who heard those men talking."

"All right," Parnell said with a nod. "I overheard two of Malone's men talking. I don't know their names, but I recognized them. They were discussing the fact that Malone had called all of his men back to his ranch. They're not blocking the trails out here to Diamondback anymore."

The Kid nodded. He had wondered how Parnell and Sophia had made it through the cordon around the ranch. The conversation Parnell had overheard explained that.

"These two men were just getting a last drink before heading out to Trident," Parnell went on. "They discussed the reason Malone is gathering his forces. He plans to launch an all-out attack on Diamondback at dawn tomorrow morning."

Owen Starbird sat up straighter in his chair. "Intends to take us by surprise, does he?"

"Yes, sir. He has close to fifty men, from what I heard. All of them hired killers, more than likely."

"More than likely," The Kid agreed. "Why are you warning us about this, Parnell?"

The newspaperman pushed his spectacles up on his nose. "Because I don't want Malone taking over the valley any more than you do. He already has everybody in town so scared they won't cross him. If he takes over Diamondback, he'll run everything in the valley, including my newspaper." Parnell shook his head. "I don't want him telling me what I can and can't print. There's still such a thing as freedom of the press, you know."

Diana said, "This is insane. Malone can't really believe that he can get away with taking over the valley and running it like some sort of feudal kingdom."

"Maybe that's not what he's really after," The Kid said. "It's not far to the border. Maybe he plans to take over just long enough to loot the whole valley and then head for Mexico before the sheriff or the Rangers can stop him. A big cleanup that'll net him a large enough fortune he can live like a king for the rest of his life."

Owen Starbird nodded and said, "Perhaps you're right, Morgan. Malone could do that and still have his revenge on me at the same time."

"He's probably planning on taking Diana with him," The Kid added.

"Well, he's going to be damn disappointed," she said sharply. "I wouldn't go to Mexico, or anywhere else, with him to save my own life."

"What about the lives of your uncle, or Gray Hawk?" The Kid suggested. "Or both of them?"

He could tell from the look in Diana's eyes that

his questions had found their target. She didn't answer, but she didn't need to. The Kid knew she *would* sacrifice herself to save the people she cared about.

"What're we gonna do?" Rocklin asked. "Now that we know Malone's gonna try to wipe us out in the mornin', we can't just sit around and wait for him to attack, can we?"

Parnell leaned forward in his chair. "If all of his men are gathered at Trident, it seems to me that it might be wise to strike at them first."

Starbird clenched a fist and nodded emphatically as he said, "I was just thinking the same thing, Mr. Parnell. In the Royal Navy, we didn't wait for the pirates to come to us. We hunted them down and destroyed them!"

"Then that's what we ought to do," Rocklin said. "Malone won't be expectin' us to hit him. As far as he knows, we still figure he's got us cut off from town."

Starbird was caught up in the excitement of strategizing. He had lost his annoying air of self-pity buoyed by the imminent prospect of action. That mood might return when he realized that he wouldn't be able to take part in the raid on Trident, but he continued to plan with Rocklin.

The Kid remained silent for the most part. Diana, Gray Hawk, Sophia, and Parnell were quiet as well. Of course, Sophia and Parnell didn't have any real part to play. They would climb into the buggy and return to Bristol after lunch. As long as Malone didn't find out that they had tried to help his enemies, they would be all right.

Starbird and Rocklin decided to hit Trident at midnight, when most of the men at the ranch would be asleep. Malone would probably have guards posted, but if they considered themselves safe they might not be too alert. Those from Diamondback had taken a strictly defensive stance, and Malone and his men had no reason to think that was going to change.

Carmelita announced that dinner was served, and once again, Diana and Sophia sat as far from each other at the dining table as they could. The Kid noticed that Parnell frowned a little at Gray Hawk, as if the idea of sitting down to eat with an Indian bothered him, but the newspaperman didn't say anything.

When the meal was over, Sophia said, "We should be getting back to town now."

"Thank you for coming out here with Mr. Parnell to warn us, Miss Kincaid," Starbird said. "You might be in danger if Malone finds out you were trying to help us."

"I stand to lose a lot more if he takes over the entire valley," she said. "Good luck to you, Captain Starbird."

She held out a gloved hand and shook with him. That put a smile on Starbird's face . . . and a frown on Diana's, The Kid noted. He drew her aside and said quietly, "You don't seem too happy about Miss Kincaid being here."

"Did you see the way she was flirting with my uncle?" Diana whispered angrily. "My God, he's three times her age!"

"I don't think he's quite that old. Twice her age, maybe. And I don't know that she was flirting. I think she was just trying to be polite."

"Maybe so, but I doubt it. And it didn't look like Uncle Owen took it that way, that's for sure."

That explained a little about Diana's attitude toward Sophia, The Kid supposed. She was afraid that Sophia might take over her place in the household. Considering the things Sophia had told him in town, The Kid was pretty sure that would never happen. Sophia seemed content where she was. But Diana might worry about that possibility anyway. When Sophia and Parnell climbed into the buggy and drove away, Diana muttered, "Good riddance."

"They came out here to help you, you know," The Kid pointed out.

"And to serve their own ends," she shot back at him.

He couldn't be sure she was wrong about that, but he had other things on his mind. The thing that had been nagging at his brain for a couple of days was becoming clearer. He just hadn't figured all of it out yet. He needed more information, but unfortunately, there was no way for him to get it short of riding to the nearest telegraph office and sending off some wires to his lawyers in San Francisco. He was sure they could burn up the telegraph wires and find out what he wanted to know, but there was no time. The attack on Malone's ranch was that night.

And The Kid had plenty to do to get ready.

Chapter 23

Excitement and anticipation gripped the ranch that afternoon and evening, as the men prepared for the raid on Malone's ranch. Rocklin stood near the corral with The Kid and said, "There are twenty-eight men in the crew. If you and the Injun come along, that'll give us thirty. Malone's bunch will still outnumber us, but we'll have the advantage of surprise on our side."

The Kid shook his head. "Gray Hawk isn't coming with us, Sam."

Rocklin stared at him in surprise for a moment before saying, "Not comin' with us? What the hell, Kid? From ever'thing I've seen and heard of that old Yaqui, I had him figured for a plumb fightin' fool."

"I suspect that's exactly what he is, but somebody has to stay here to keep an eye on Diana and her uncle. I asked Gray Hawk to do that."

Rocklin's frown deepened. "You reckon this is a trick of some sort?"

"I don't know, but we have to be aware that it might be."

The foreman nodded slowly. "Yeah, I guess you could be right. We don't want to leave the cap'n and Miss Diana here without anybody to watch out for 'em."

It would take about an hour to ride from Diamondback to Trident. Rocklin knew the way and would lead the attack. The Starbird ranch hands gathered at the corral at ten o'clock to saddle their horses. That would give them enough time to reach their destination, make any plans that needed to be made once they had scouted out the situation, and get into position for the raid.

The Kid was in the living room of the ranch house, about to leave the house to join Rocklin and the others, when Owen Starbird appeared, being pushed in his wheelchair by Diana. Carmelita trailed behind them, carrying Starbird's crutches.

"Captain," The Kid said, nodding to the older man. "Come to wish us luck?"

"Help me outside, Morgan," Starbird said as he put his hands on the arms of the chair to push himself to his feet. "I want to talk to the men before they leave."

The Kid stepped forward to steady Starbird while Diana moved up on his other side to lend a hand. Carmelita took the crutches to him. Starbird tucked them under his arms and gripped the handles tightly.

Even with The Kid and Diana to help him, the muscles in Starbird's neck stood out like cords as he struggled against the drag of his useless legs. He clumped over to the door. Carmelita held it open for him. The struggle continued across the porch and down the steps to the ground.

Rocklin saw them coming. "Quiet down, you varmints," he snapped at the crew, who were talking and laughing among themselves, excited over the prospect of taking the fight to the men who'd been tormenting them for weeks.

There was an undercurrent of nervousness in their voices, too, The Kid thought. They all knew that they were going to face danger. A lot of bullets would fly, and it was highly likely that not everyone who rode away from the ranch would come back alive.

Starbird made his slow, torturous way toward the corral as silence fell. The light from a three-quarter moon washed over the faces of the punchers as they turned toward him. Starbird finally came to a stop in front of them, his chest rising and falling heavily as he breathed hard from his exertions. He had to wait a moment to recover a little before he could speak.

"Men, I want you to know how very proud I am of each and every one of you. You've been faithful lads despite the odds against you. You've risked your lives, and others have . . . have given their lives. Some have suffered injuries protecting this ranch. I appreciate your loyalty and your gallantry more than I can possibly say."

"Shoot, boss, we know that," Rocklin said. "We're just doin' our jobs. We ride for the brand."

"Darn right," one of the men added. "Like Sam says, we ride for the brand."

The others joined in a chorus of agreement.

"Be that as it may," Starbird said when things had quieted down again, "what I am going to ask of you now goes above and beyond the call of duty."

Rocklin shook his head. "Not hardly. We're lookin' forward to fightin' that blasted Malone and his bunch o' pirates and gun-wolves, ain't we, fellas?"

That question brought a lusty cheer from the assembled punchers.

"No, no," Starbird said stubbornly. "It's more than that. I've been thinking a great deal about how you need to proceed tonight."

The Kid looked behind Starbird's back at Diana and frowned quizzically. She gave a tiny shake of her head to indicate that she didn't know what her uncle was talking about, either.

Rocklin frowned, too. He said, "Maybe you best explain what you're gettin' at, Cap'n. We're still gonna ride over to Trident and give Malone hell and hot lead, ain't we?"

"Indeed you are," Starbird said, "but only if he refuses to surrender."

Everyone was silent for a couple of seconds, as if

they couldn't believe what they had just heard. Then Rocklin burst out, "Surrender! I thought we were gonna just fill the sons o'—I mean, the polecats—full of holes!"

"Although this isn't England, this is still a civilized country, a land of law and order," Starbird insisted. "We have no official standing beyond that of citizens, but we are acting in the right by opposing Malone, and therefore are justified in taking whatever measures are necessary to stop him from threatening the peace and security of everyone in the valley. But in order for our actions to have any legitimacy, we must proceed in a proper manner. We must call on Malone to surrender, for him and his men to put down their arms and submit themselves to the proper authority. I'm sure the Rangers will arrive sooner or later, and they can see to it that Malone and his men are tried in a court of law."

The Kid was surprised to hear Starbird talking like that. He had thought the man understood how things were done out here. He thought that Diamondback had been attacked enough to make Starbird realize they had to fight back. Starbird could talk about law and order all he wanted to, but there came a time when the only law that counted came in calibers.

At the same time, the change of heart on Starbird's part wasn't totally unexpected. After all, Starbird had been an officer in the Royal Navy and had captained his own ship. There were certain ways of doing things, and those methods were drummed into him. They were part of him. He couldn't ignore them. When he had finally captured Black Terence Malone, Starbird hadn't killed the dreaded pirate or his crew, The Kid reminded himself. He had taken them back to England so that they could be put on trial and thrown into prison where they belonged.

The Kid knew in every fiber of his being that Malone wouldn't surrender. But in calling on him to do so, as Starbird wanted, the men from Diamondback would be giving up the advantage of surprise.

Sam Rocklin knew it, too. "That ain't a smart thing to do, boss," he argued. "If we let Malone know we're there, he and his men will have a chance to fort up. We got to get right among 'em and hit 'em fast and hard, so we can whittle down the odds before they know what's goin' on. Otherwise . . ."

Rocklin didn't finish the sentence, but The Kid knew what he meant. Without the element of surprise on their side, Malone and his men might be able to wipe them out. Malone would suffer some casualties, too, no doubt about that, but in the end he would win.

"I'm sorry, Sam," Starbird said. "You're a good man and true, and I know that I'm asking a great deal of you and the lads. But if our victory is to mean anything, if we're to emerge from this with our honor intact, you simply must do as I wish."

Rocklin looked at his employer for a long

moment. The silence stretched out. Then, abruptly, Rocklin jerked his head in a nod.

"If that's the way you want it, boss," he said, "that's the way it'll be."

Some of the punchers started to protest. Rocklin's head jerked around toward them and he silenced them with a cold stare.

"Thank you, Sam," Starbird said. "Are you ready to depart?"

"Yes, sir, we sure are. I don't know when we'll be back. We may have to lay siege to the place to smoke out all them rats."

"Do whatever you need to." Starbird held out his hand. "And good luck to you. Each and every man jack of you." The two of them shook hands.

Starbird turned and held out his hand to The Kid as well. "This still isn't your fight, Morgan, unless you choose for it to be," he said.

The Kid gripped the older man's strong hand. "It was my fight the minute I first laid eyes on Malone and his lowdown bunch," he said.

"Very well. Thank you, my young friend."

"I'll help you back to the house, and then I can join Sam and the others—"

"Carmelita and Diana can help me," Starbird said.

"You're sure?"

"Quite."

The Kid nodded. "All right." He had already saddled the buckskin and put the horse with the others. The Winchester and the Sharps rode snug in their sheaths. The Kid moved over and took the reins from the cowboy who'd been holding them.

"Mount up!" Rocklin called.

The Kid swung up into the saddle and the others did likewise. Rocklin touched the brim of his hat in a sort of salute as he led the group past Starbird, Diana, and Carmelita. They kept the horses at a slow walk so as not to kick up a bunch of dust.

The Kid nodded to Diana as he rode past her. He saw the fear on her face and knew that some of it was for him, although he was sure she was worried about all the Diamondback hands. She was fiery and impulsive at times, but he had grown fond of her in the few days he had known her. It seemed that she felt the same way about him.

Someday, if he ever found himself in a similar situation, he might be able to entertain thoughts about settling down again.

But that day hadn't arrived yet. Not by a long shot. He was willing to risk his life for Diana and her uncle and their ranch, but when it was all over, if he was still alive he would ride away without looking back. He knew that.

And judging by the bittersweet smile on Diana's face, so did she.

They left the ranch headquarters behind, riding off into the night toward the river and the Trident ranch beyond it. The Kid brought the buckskin up alongside Rocklin's mount.

"Are you really going to do what Captain Starbird asked you to do?"

Rocklin grunted. "It pains the hell outta me to say it, Kid, but . . . hell, no. Might as well put our guns to our heads and blow our own brains out as to give Malone a chance, the way he outnumbers us. He'll be on his own stompin' grounds, too. Onliest chance we got is to take them bastards by surprise."

"So you lied to the captain."

"I done what I had to, damn it!" Rocklin blew his breath out in exasperation. "We'll tell the cap'n that we done what he said and that Malone refused to surrender. That's what he's expectin' to hear, and to tell the truth, it's what would happen anyway if we did follow the cap'n's orders. Difference is, doin' it his way, we'd likely all be dead 'fore the night's over, and then there wouldn't be anybody left to save the old man and the girl from Malone. He'd kill the cap'n, and as for Miss Diana . . . well, I don't have to tell you what he's got in mind for her, Kid."

"No, you don't," The Kid agreed. "And for what it's worth, Sam, I think you're doin' the right thing."

Rocklin sighed. "It's sure as hell hard to protect somebody when they're always lookin' over your shoulder, bitchin' about the way you have to go about it, especially when they don't know how bad the things out there in the dark really are."

"Yeah, I imagine it's a thankless chore," The Kid said. "Somebody's got to do it, though."

"Yeah, and it looks like we're elected." Rocklin glanced over at him. "Glad you're comin' along for the ruckus, Kid. Even takin' those varmints by surprise, I got a hunch we're gonna need all the help we can get."

The Kid couldn't argue with that.

Chapter 24

Twenty-nine men on horseback couldn't move through the night without making some noise, but the group from Diamondback rode as quietly as possible once they had crossed the Severn River, just in case Malone had any scouts out. Sam Rocklin had lived in the valley for a long time and knew every foot of the trails, so The Kid was happy to let the ramrod lead the way.

It was a little after eleven o'clock when they approached the headquarters of Malone's ranch. According to Rocklin, they had been on Trident range almost since crossing the river. They were closing in on the old ranch house and the other outbuildings.

Rocklin reined in atop a wooded hill that overlooked the ranch. In the moonlight, The Kid saw a spawling, single-story house that had probably started out as a small cabin. It had been expanded by building additions to it in rather haphazard fashion. Beyond it were the barns, the corrals, the long, low bunkhouse, and a small blacksmith shop. Rocklin pointed them out to The Kid.

"Seems like you know the place pretty well," The Kid commented.

"I used to be over here quite a bit when old Silas Wilmott owned the place," Rocklin explained. "Him and George got along well and did some business together."

"George Starbird, Diana's father?"

"Yeah." Rocklin chuckled. "Funny how he was always just George to me, even though he was the boss, no doubt about that, but the cap'n's always been the cap'n. For brothers, they weren't much alike. George was just as plain and simple as he could be, didn't put on no airs and would get out and work alongside the hands just like he was a forty-a-month-and-found puncher, too. I ain't sayin' nothin' bad about the cap'n, mind you. He's just different from his brother, that's all." Rocklin glanced over. "You got a brother, Kid?"

"Not that I know of."

"Me, neither." Rocklin took a deep breath. "All right. We'll spread out so that we've got the whole place surrounded. Then we'll close in." He started naming off punchers and telling them where to go, assigning more men to the bunkhouse than anywhere else. He concluded by saying, "I'm goin' in the house after Malone."

"I'm coming with you," The Kid said.

Rocklin grinned. "Glad to hear it. I was just gettin' to that. He's liable to have Wolfram in there with him, maybe Breck and Early that you had the run-in with, too. Now that Greavy's dead, those three are his right-hand men." The foreman turned to the others. "I'll give everybody plenty of time to get in position. If you run into any of Malone's men, try to kill 'em as quick and quiet-like as you can. But if you have to shoot, do it. If all hell breaks loose, that'll be the go-ahead, boys. Rush in there and blast as many of 'em as you can, as fast as you can. Otherwise, wait for my signal. That'll be three shots, fired fast. When you hear 'em, let the rat-killin' commence."

The assembled cowboys nodded grimly in understanding. The jovial, excited atmosphere they had shared earlier had disappeared as they recognized they were going about the solemn task of defending their home ranch.

The men split up, spreading out around Trident headquarters. Soon The Kid and Rocklin were alone on top of the hill. They dismounted. From there they would go on foot, stealing up on their enemies like Indians.

Quietly, The Kid said, "You know, some people would consider what you're about to do to be murder."

Rocklin snorted in disgust. "Yeah, and some people don't know their rumps from a hole in the ground. Malone and his bunch have run roughshod over the valley. They've killed innocent folks, destroyed property, and acted like they can raise all the hell they want to without ever havin' to answer for it. It ain't murder to wipe out a pack of wolves, is it?"

"I never said it was," The Kid replied with a smile. He had wiped out a few human wolf packs before, and never lost a minute's sleep over sending some evil sons of bitches straight to the hell they deserved. Well, not too much sleep.

"Good." Rocklin drew his gun. "Let's go set things right."

They started down the hill, moving swiftly and silently, using all the cover they could find in case Malone had guards posted. Heading straight for the house, The Kid and Rocklin reached it in about ten minutes. As they paused fifty yards from the front porch and crouched behind the stone wall around a well, Rocklin pointed at himself and then at the front door. He pointed at The Kid and made a circling motion, indicating that The Kid should go around to the back. The Kid nodded his understanding. Rocklin held up two fingers indicating two minutes, and The Kid nodded again.

Rocklin mouthed, *Good luck*, and the two men split up. The Kid crouched low and ran around the house. He drew his Colt and held it ready for action. The night was still quiet. The lack of gunfire meant either that the Diamondback punchers hadn't run into any of Malone's men, or they'd been able to dispatch the enemy without shooting.

It was only right that they had a little luck, The Kid thought. Not only were they outnumbered, but most of Malone's men were professional gunmen who were highly efficient at killing. The men from Diamondback were cowboys. Tough, rugged hombres, sure, and many of them were no strangers to violence, but still, they weren't the same sort as Malone's crew. That's why it was absolutely necessary for them to take Malone's men by surprise. Even with that going for them, The Kid expected that they might take heavy losses.

He paused at the rear corner of the house and pressed his back against the wall for a second as he listened intently. If anyone was lurking behind the ranch house, they were doing so in complete silence. The Kid wheeled around the corner and headed for the back door. He'd been counting off the seconds in his head and knew that a little more than a minute and a half had passed since he and Rocklin split up. In less than thirty seconds, Rocklin would be entering the house.

The Kid reached the door. If it was locked or barred from inside, he would have to find some other way in, probably through a window. When he tried the latch, though, it opened. A faint smile tugged at his mouth in the darkness. Malone didn't expect any trouble in his own home.

The former pirate was about to find out just how wrong that assumption was.

The Kid swung the door back slowly, hoping that the hinges wouldn't creak. They did, but only faintly. The noise was so soft it couldn't be heard more than a few feet away. The Kid went into the house fast, crouching low to make himself a smaller target. His Colt swept from side to side, ready to blast back if an enemy's muzzle flash ripped through the shadows.

Nothing flashed. The house was dark and quiet. The Kid straightened. His keen ears strained to hear anything.

Three gunshots suddenly roared at the front of the house so loud they were like fists against The Kid's ears. From outside, more shots rang out in response to Rocklin's signal, and men shouted wildly, loosing rebel yells designed to startle and disorient their enemies. The Kid's eyes had adjusted to the darkness and he ran down a hallway. He kicked open a door at the end, figuring it probably led to a bedroom, maybe even Malone's.

The room was dark and empty. The Kid saw a big bed and knew he had guessed right, but nobody was there.

Footsteps pounded in the corridor behind him. He whirled around and spotted a familiar shape. A gun in the man's hand lifted toward him.

"Sam, hold your fire!" The Kid called. "It's me! Morgan!"

Rocklin lowered his gun. "Kid? What the hell? Where is ever'body?"

"There's no one in the front of the house?"

"Nobody!"

"Let's check the other rooms," The Kid suggested. It took only a minute and the search confirmed what The Kid had already begun to suspect. The Trident ranch house was unoccupied.

The shooting from outside had died away quickly, he realized. As he headed for the front door, he said, "Let's see what the rest of the boys found."

"I got a bad feelin' about this, Kid," Rocklin said.

The Kid's voice was bleak as he said, "Me, too."

They stepped onto the porch, and in the moon-light they saw men milling around the bunkhouse, the barns, and the corrals. A couple of the men trotted toward the main house, and one of them called, "Hey, Sam! There's nobody here!"

"You looked ever'where?" Rocklin asked.

"Yeah, just about," the puncher replied as he and his companion came up to the porch. "I reckon there could still be one or two of Malone's varmints hidin' somewhere, but I kinda doubt it."

"So do I," said The Kid. "It appears that Malone and all of his men have left here."

"But if that's true," Rocklin said, "then where in blazes did they go?"

One possible answer to that occurred to The Kid and Rocklin at the same time. Rocklin exclaimed, "Diamondback!"

"Let's get the horses," The Kid said in an urgent, worried voice. He holstered his gun and bounded down the steps from the ranch house porch.

Rocklin was right behind him. The foreman began to yell, "Ever'body come on! Back to the horses! Back to the ranch!"

As The Kid hurried up the hill toward the spot where they had left their mounts, he thought about Jefferson Parnell. Sophia hadn't heard the conversation between Malone's men that Parnell had reported. They had only the newspaperman's word for what he had overheard. Parnell could have lied to Sophia and to the rest of them as well.

But why would he do such a thing? Had he decided that he was going to knuckle under to Malone and help the former pirate get his revenge on Owen Starbird? It was possible, The Kid decided. The promise of money or the threat of death were both effective persuaders, even more so when they were combined. Despite Parnell's pose as an honest newspaperman, The Kid could see him selling out to Malone.

They would know in an hour or so, he thought as the men reached the horses. The Kid grabbed the reins and swung up into the saddle on the buckskin's back. All around him, the Diamondback punchers were mounting up as well. "Let's go!" Rocklin shouted again. "Come on!"

Hoofbeats filled the night like thunder as the men rode out, fear and desperation fueling the hard gallop toward the Severn River and Diamondback range beyond.

Chapter 25

The riders didn't attempt to travel quietly. They rode hard for Diamondback, splashing across the river and hitting the trail that would take them to the headquarters of the ranch.

The more The Kid thought about it, the more convinced he was that Malone had tricked them, with the assistance of Jefferson Parnell. Knowing that Starbird would want to strike first if he found out that Malone was planning a dawn raid on the ranch, Malone had figured that the whole Diamondback crew would head for Trident that night, leaving Starbird and Diana unprotected.

Well, unprotected except for Gray Hawk and Carmelita, he amended, but he knew the old Yaqui and the servant wouldn't be any match for Malone's ruthless hired guns. Diana would put up a fight, too, but it wouldn't be enough—not nearly enough.

Starbird and Gray Hawk might be dead, and

Diana could easily be a prisoner in Malone's hands. That thought made The Kid's jaw clench tightly.

He would avenge them, he vowed . . . but he knew from bitter experience just how hollow revenge could be. It never brought back the ones who'd been lost.

As they approached Diamondback headquarters, The Kid reined in and motioned for Rocklin to do likewise. As the two men brought their horses to a halt, the rest of the punchers followed suit.

"What is it?" Rocklin snapped. "I want to find out if the cap'n and Miss Diana are all right."

"So do I," The Kid said, "but if we go charging in there blindly, we might be riding right into a trap."

Rocklin thought about it for a second and then jerked his head in a nod. "Yeah, you're right," he admitted. "Malone could have his men waitin' to cut loose at us."

"All of you stay here. I'll slip in there and find out what's going on."

"Sounds like a good way to get yourself killed, Kid."

"I'll run that risk," The Kid said. "If it's all clear, I'll light a lantern, come out in front of the house, and swing it back and forth over my head three times. You should be able to see that signal from here."

"We'll be waitin'," Rocklin promised. "But if we hear any shots, we're headin' on in, hellbent-for-leather."

The Kid grinned. "Good idea, because if you hear any shots, I could probably use some help."

He left the rest of the riders there and headed toward the house. When he estimated that he was within a quarter mile, he dismounted and continued on foot, moving as stealthily as he could. Frank Morgan could slip in and out of an enemy camp without anyone ever knowing he'd been there, but The Kid wasn't that good yet. He was working on it, though. Maybe someday he'd be able to hold a candle to The Drifter in all the ways that really counted.

If he lived long enough.

A few lights burned in the house. The Kid paused under some trees and watched the place closely, waiting to see if any shadows moved in front of the lights. After a moment, one did. Somebody was in there, all right, but he didn't know who it was.

He listened intently as well. If Malone's men were hidden around the ranch, waiting to ambush the Diamondback punchers when they returned, their horses had to be somewhere. The Kid didn't hear any soft whinnies, or the stamping of hooves. Maybe the horses had been led off out of earshot.

He was also alert for the smell of tobacco. Ambushes had been ruined in the past by some thoughtless hombre firing up a quirly. Even if he hid the coal at the end of the cigarette, the smell would be a giveaway.

There was no tobacco smell. Could it be that

the ranch was really as quiet and peaceful as it appeared? Had he been wrong about the trickery he suspected on Malone's part?

The Kid's gaze fastened on the living room window where he had seen the shadow of someone moving around and where yellow lamplight continued to glow. He had to get a look through that window.

Gripping his Colt tightly, The Kid dashed across the open ground between the trees and the porch. He vaulted directly onto the porch, landing lightly enough so that whoever was inside might not have heard him. He put his back to the wall and slid along it toward the window.

When he was only inches away, he took off his hat and leaned closer, edging an eye past the window frame to peer through the opening. The pane was raised because it was a warm night. He was able to hear the slight grunt Carmelita made as she drew a bandage tight around Gray Hawk's left arm.

The Kid stiffened. No one else was in the room except the Yaqui and the woman. That didn't mean the coast was clear. Malone and his men could be elsewhere in the house.

Carmelita spoke in Spanish. The Kid understood the language well enough to know that she was telling Gray Hawk the bleeding had stopped. "*Bueno*," the Yaqui said. "I must find Señor Morgan and tell him what happened here."

They wouldn't be talking so calmly if Malone was still lurking around, The Kid decided. He stepped to the door and swung it open, saying, "You won't have to find me, Gray Hawk. I'm here."

At The Kid's entrance, Gray Hawk's hand had started toward the rifle that lay on the table next to him. He stopped before snatching up the weapon and came sharply to his feet.

"Señor," he said.

"Where are Captain Starbird and Señorita Diana?" The Kid asked. The question made Carmelita cover her face with her hands, and he saw her shoulders begin to shake a little as she cried.

"Gone," Gray Hawk replied. "The pirate man has them."

"Malone?"

Gray Hawk nodded. "He and his men came a short time ago. I could not stop them from breaking in and taking El Capitán and the señorita. There were too many of them."

"I know," The Kid said. "How bad are you hurt?"

Gray Hawk glanced down at the bandage on his arm and shook his head contemptuously. "A scratch, nothing more. I heard them coming and thought you and the others had returned sooner than expected, but when I went out to see, they opened fire on me. I could not get back to the house, so I took cover in the barn. Malone and some of his men went into the house and brought out El Capitán and Señorita Diana. I could not shoot for fear of hitting them."

The Kid nodded. "I understand. I'm surprised they left you alive."

"The one called Wolfram wanted to burn down the barn with me inside it, but Malone ordered that I be left alone. He wanted to leave me alive so I could deliver a message to you, señor. He said he is taking the prisoners to the settlement called Bristol. There he will await you at dawn tomorrow. You can go and try to take them back . . . or you and all the Diamondback men can leave Rattlesnake Valley forever."

"Leave it to him, that's what he means," The Kid said. "He's holding them hostage to force us to either abandon the valley or ride into a trap where he can wipe us out."

Gray Hawk's head bobbed up and down. "Sí, señor. This is what I believe as well."

The Kid frowned as he said, "But if he knew we were coming to Trident tonight, why didn't he just set a trap for us there, like I figured he might be doing? This business of kidnapping Diana and her uncle doesn't make any sense."

Gray Hawk just stared expressionlessly at him. The Yaqui obviously didn't have any answers, either.

A couple of things were clear, though: The Kid

couldn't ride off and leave the valley to Malone, nor could he allow Diana and Starbird to remain prisoners. He had to free them somehow and then deal with Malone.

He went over to a table where a lamp burned and picked it up. As he started toward the front door, he asked, "Do you think Malone was surprised when he found Diamondback deserted tonight, Gray Hawk?"

"From things I heard him say to the one called Wolfram, I think that is true, señor."

The Kid was left wondering again what part Jefferson Parnell was playing. He had been convinced that Parnell had been doing Malone's bidding when he decoyed them to Trident, even though that didn't fit in with the other theory The Kid had been mulling over in his brain. He didn't know what to believe.

He went out to the yard. Lifting the lamp over his head, he moved it back and forth three times, as he had told Rocklin he would. That signal would bring the foreman and the rest of the Diamondback crew galloping toward the ranch.

By the time The Kid got back inside and set the lamp on the table, he heard hoofbeats approaching the house. He motioned for Gray Hawk to follow him and stepped back onto the porch as the riders galloped up and pulled their mounts to a halt. A large cloud of dust swirled around them for a moment before the night breezes began to carry it off.

"Where are they?" Rocklin demanded.

"Gone," The Kid said. "Malone and his bunch showed up here earlier and took Captain Starbird and Diana to Bristol."

"Bristol!" the foreman repeated. "Why would he take 'em to the settlement?"

"I wondered about that, too. The only reason I can see is that Malone wants to have the final showdown there because we'll have to worry about the citizens getting caught in the crossfire."

Rocklin snorted in disgust. "You can bet Malone and the rest of those varmints won't be worryin' about that!"

"I know," The Kid said with a nod. "Malone figures it'll be one more advantage for him."

"Well . . . I reckon he might be right." Rocklin shook his head. "We can't just charge in there with all guns a-blazin'. Too many innocent folks'd get hurt. I ain't got much use for most o' them townies, the way they been toadyin' up to Malone, but we can't just shoot 'em down, neither."

"And Malone knows that." The Kid rubbed his jaw as he frowned in thought. "Malone's given us a deadline of dawn. We either ride into his trap and try to rescue the prisoners, or we leave the valley."

"Leave the valley? That'd mean givin' up!"

"That's right. What we need is a third option."

Rocklin leaned forward in his saddle, crossed

his hand on the horn, and sighed heavily. "If you got any ideas, Kid, I'd sure like to hear 'em."

"Right now I don't," The Kid said as he shook his head.

That was when Gray Hawk stepped forward and said, "Perhaps there is something I can do."

Chapter 26

Two hours later, Sam Rocklin paced impatiently up and down the ranch house porch, pausing every now and then to peer off into the darkness. It was long after midnight. The moon had set, and the night was stygian, the thick black relieved only by the faint glow of millions of stars overhead.

The Kid sat nearby in a ladderback chair, leaning back with one foot propped on the porch railing. He flexed the muscles in his leg and made the chair rock slightly.

"Might as well take it easy, Sam," The Kid advised.

The foreman turned sharply toward him. "How in Hades can I do that, knowin' that the boss and that poor gal are bein' held prisoner by a skunk like Malone? There's no tellin' what that varmint might do, Kid!"

"I don't think he'll hurt them. He needs them as

hostages right now, until he sees what we're going to do."

"How about when it gets to be dawn and we ain't showed up?" Rocklin wanted to know. "What happens then?"

"We'll be there," The Kid said. "Gray Hawk told us that he'd be back in plenty of time."

He wished he felt as confident as he sounded. His instincts told him that he could trust Gray Hawk, but he had only known the old Yaqui for a short time. It was possible he could be wrong about him.

"What do you reckon that redskin's up to, anyway?" Rocklin asked.

The Kid shook his head. "I don't know. All I know is he said he had an idea how he could help us."

"Yeah, well, I hope he ain't gone back to the mountains to squat in that cave o' his and pray to some heathen spirits—holy cow!"

The startled exclamation from Rocklin made The Kid leap to his feet. His hand moved instinctively toward his gun before he stopped the draw. He stepped to the railing and looked out at the sight that had jarred the words out of the foreman.

Gray Hawk had returned . . . and he wasn't alone.

The Kid and Rocklin hadn't heard the Yaqui come up to the ranch house. The area in front of the house was empty one second, and the next, two dozen figures filled it as if they had appeared by magic.

Or maybe they were ghosts. The Kid knew that was a crazy thought even as it went through his head, but it was there anyway. The white-clad figures certainly looked like phantoms, and obviously they moved with the silence of the dead.

Gray Hawk stood in front with the others scattered behind him. He held out a hand, waving it toward his companions, and said, "The young men of my people have come to help."

"Yaquis," Rocklin muttered. "Son of a bitch."

His hand moved toward the gun on his hip. The Kid gripped his arm and stopped him.

"Hold it, Sam," he murmured. "Gray Hawk said they've come to help."

"Yeah, but they're Yaquis!" Rocklin protested. "You don't know what savages they are, Kid!"

"Worse than Malone and his pirates and hired killers?"

Rocklin frowned. "Folks out here used to live in mortal fear of those redskins."

"That was the past. Let me talk to Gray Hawk."

Rocklin muttered something else under his breath but stayed where he was as The Kid stepped off the porch. He nodded to Gray Hawk and said, "Thank you for the help you've brought to us, amigo."

"You aided me when Malone tried to capture me," Gray Hawk said with his usual solemn dignity. "And the señorita and her uncle have always been kind, as her father was before them. They see to it that Gray Hawk is left alone. Now, I can help them."

The Kid nodded toward the other shadowy figures. "How did you get them here so fast? You haven't had time to make it to the border and back, even on a fast horse, and I didn't think there were any more of your people on this side of the Rio Grande."

"There are ways of summoning that do not require a horse," Gray Hawk replied, and The Kid thought he heard just a trace of unaccustomed humor in the old man's voice.

"I'll take your word for it," The Kid said, knowing that it might be better not to probe too deeply into the secrets of the Yaqui. Anyway, it was possible that a whole band of them were living in those rugged mountains to the west without any of the inhabitants of Rattlesnake Valley knowing about it. Just because people assumed that all the Yaquis had fled to Mexico didn't mean it was true.

The Kid settled for saying, "Thank you. What do you suggest we do now?"

Gray Hawk said, "My people can move in the shadows without being seen. We will go to Bristol, slip into the settlement, and find El Capitán and Señorita Diana. We can free them and get them out of town, so that when you and Señor Rocklin and the others attack at the rising of the sun, they will be safe. We can help you battle the evil ones as well, since we will already be in their midst."

That could work, The Kid thought as he

considered Gray Hawk's words. With the Yaquis added to the Diamondback punchers, the odds against Malone's men would be just about even. If the Yaquis could take Malone by surprise, which The Kid didn't doubt was possible considering the way they had slipped up on the ranch, that would swing the advantage to their side. They might be able to overwhelm Malone's forces without the whole town getting caught in the middle of a huge shootout.

The plan needed one modification, though.

"I'm coming with you," The Kid said.

"A white man cannot move like a Yaqui."

"Maybe not, but I'm coming anyway. I have to make sure that Diana is safe."

Gray Hawk's face and voice were impassive, but The Kid thought he heard a hint of annoyance anyway as the Yaqui asked, "You do not trust us?"

"It's not a matter of trust," The Kid insisted. "I just want to know that she's out of danger before the rest of the shooting starts."

For a moment, Gray Hawk stood there in silence. Then, abruptly, he nodded.

"But if you jeopardize the señorita, you will answer to Gray Hawk," he added.

"Fine by me," The Kid said. "When do we leave?"

"Now. It will be dawn in less than three hours."

The Kid turned to Rocklin, who still stood on the porch. "Did you hear all of that, Sam?"

"I heard it," Rocklin replied. "We'll be ridin' in at

dawn, Kid. I expect all hell will break loose when we do. I just hope you and them heathens are in position to give us a hand when that happens, otherwise we may not stand much of a chance against Malone's bunch."

"We'll be there," The Kid promised.

Some of the men had grabbed a little sleep after getting back from Trident, while others were too keyed up to doze off and had been awake all night. The Kid fell into that category and he wasn't feeling sleepy as he put his saddle back on the buckskin and got ready to head for Bristol with the Yaquis.

Rocklin had followed The Kid into the barn. "Don't trust those savages too much," he advised. "They'll turn on you without any warnin' if you give 'em half a chance."

The Kid shook his head. "I don't think so. Gray Hawk feels like he owes me, and he's grateful to Diana and her uncle, too. I believe he can be trusted, and the others will do what he says."

"How do you know that? You reckon he's their chief or something?"

"I don't know about that, but they came when he summoned them, didn't they? They wouldn't have done that if they didn't respect him."

"Maybe so," Rocklin said grudgingly. "Just be careful, Kid."

"I intend to. For one thing, I want to get Diana out of there safely."

Rocklin studied him in the feeble light of the one lantern that was lit, with its flame turned down low. He said, "I'm thinkin' that if we can get all this business with Malone took care of, you might want to coil your lass' rope here for a while, Kid. This valley will be a mighty nice place to live once Malone's gone. Well, except for havin' to keep your eyes open for rattlers, that is. But I reckon Miss Diana would like it if you was to stay. She's got a sharp tongue sometimes, but her heart's as big as all o' Texas and she could use a good man around."

The Kid drew the cinches tight on his saddle and smiled faintly as he shook his head. "That's not going to happen, Sam. I want the business with Malone settled as much as you do, but once it is, I'll be riding on. If there hadn't been trouble here, I'd have been gone already."

"Is that what you do?" Rocklin snapped. "Just ride around lookin' for trouble?"

"No, but sometimes I think trouble looks for me."

To tell the truth, The Kid *didn't* know what he was looking for with his endless drifting. Ever since Rebel's death, he had found no answers, and he wasn't even sure what the questions were anymore. All he knew was that he couldn't stay in any one place for long, and he never got too close to anyone. He would help people who needed his help, but that was all it amounted to. If that meant he was actually looking for trouble, then so be it.

In the end, he was still a loner. Maybe he always would be.

With that bitter thought in his head, he shoved the Winchester in its sheath, then reached for the Sharps. He didn't know if he would need either of the long guns—if he had to fight in Bristol, no doubt it would be at close quarters—but it wouldn't hurt anything to take them with him.

Ready to go, he led the buckskin out of the barn. Gray Hawk was waiting for him, but the rest of the Yaquis were gone.

"Where are the others?" The Kid asked.

"Nearby," Gray Hawk replied. "They will follow us to the settlement."

"You know your way to town?"

Again there was a trace of amusement in the old Indian's voice as he said, "Gray Hawk knows every foot of this valley."

"Well, then, I'm ready if you are. Where's your horse?"

Gray Hawk gave a little whistle, and his pinto trotted out of the trees. Both men swung up onto their mounts.

The Kid lifted a hand in farewell to Rocklin. "See you at dawn, Sam."

"We'll be there," the ramrod promised grimly.

The Kid and Gray Hawk rode out, leaving Diamondback behind. The Yaqui took the lead, although The Kid rode alongside him. When they

were about half a mile from the ranch, The Kid
heard the sound of hoofbeats and glanced back,
and sure enough, the other Yaquis were there,
riding nimble little ponies like Gray Hawk's, although not all of them were pintos. The Kid hadn't
heard them come up behind him and his companion, but the important thing was that they were
there.

As they rode toward Bristol, The Kid kept an eye
on the sky. The heavens were still black, filled with
an awesome, sweeping display of brilliantly shining and twinkling stars, but along the eastern horizon in front of them, the faintest tinge of gray was
visible above the hills that formed the boundary
at that end of the valley. That tiny glow was a har-
binger of the approaching dawn. He and Gray
Hawk wouldn't have very long to locate and rescue
Diana and Starbird before the sun came up and
brought with it the sound of guns. An hour at most,
The Kid estimated.

He wondered where Malone would be holding
the prisoners, and even as he pondered that question, a possible answer sprang into his mind. The
Rattler's Den was pretty much in the center of the
settlement, and it was one of the biggest buildings
in town. The Kid thought that the idea of swagger-
ing into the saloon, taking it over, and making it his
headquarters would appeal to Black Terence
Malone. That might be a good place to start looking, anyway.

Something else occurred to him. He turned to

Gray Hawk and asked, "Tell me about the eastern end of the valley."

If the question struck the Yaqui as odd, he didn't say anything about it. Instead, he said, "What do you want to know, señor?"

"Yesterday when I was up in the mountains near your cave, I looked down the valley, and it appeared that the gap at the far end is on about the same level as the pass."

Gray Hawk nodded. "This is true. The valley is deeper at the western end and generally slopes upward from west to east. The slope is gentle, though, and not easily noticed."

"How wide is the gap that leads through the hills to the desert?"

Gray Hawk pondered that question for a moment before replying, "A man could shoot an arrow from one side to the other without any trouble."

"Is there any other good way through the hills?"

Gray Hawk shook his head. "A man could ride over them, but they are steep and rocky. It would not be easy. Why do you want to know these things, señor? They have nothing to do with the pirate man."

"Maybe not," The Kid said.

But he was starting to believe that they had a lot to do with the things that had been happening in Rattlesnake Valley.

Chapter 27

It looked like every lamp and lantern in the settlement had been lit. The lights of Bristol glittered in the predawn darkness and cast a glow in the sky above the town. Bonfires burned here and there in the streets as well.

The Kid and Gray Hawk regarded the settlement from the top of a shallow hill about half a mile away. Gray Hawk made a sound like he had bitten into something that tasted bad.

"Malone is taking no chances," the Yaqui said. "He wants to be able to see if anyone tries to sneak up on him."

"That's going to make it harder for us to get in there," The Kid said.

"Harder . . . but not impossible."

The Kid smiled in the darkness. "No, not impossible."

Gray Hawk went back to the waiting Yaquis and spoke to them in hurried Spanish, too swiftly for

The Kid to follow. Then they split up, vanishing into the night as silently as they had first appeared. The Kid wasn't sure how they managed to blend in with the shadows wearing those light-colored clothes, but somehow they were able to do it.

When Gray Hawk rejoined him, The Kid said, "I thought we'd head for the Rattler's Den. That's a saloon in the middle of town. It would be a good place for Malone to hole up."

Gray Hawk nodded. "You know more about the town than I do, señor. Señorita Diana brings me the few supplies that I need. I have been there, but not often."

"I'll lead the way, then. We'll have to see if we can reach the alley behind the saloon and get in that way."

They left their horses behind and stole toward the settlement. As they drew closer, The Kid heard the faint strains of a player piano's notes floating through the air. It was a melancholy tune, not quite a funeral dirge but almost, and for a moment it threatened to unnerve him.

Then he saw something that stiffened his resolve as anger coursed through him.

Someone had planted a pole in the middle of the street in front of the Rattler's Den, and in the light that spilled through the windows along the street, The Kid saw a flag attached to that pole. It flapped gently in the breeze, standing out just enough for him to see what was emblazoned on it.

The skull and crossbones. A pirate flag.

Since it was right in front of the Rattler's Den, The Kid was more sure than ever that he would find Black Terence Malone in there, along with the prisoners. The flag was a challenge, a defiant slap in the face to anyone who dared to oppose Malone.

The Kid pointed it out to Gray Hawk as they crouched behind an old abandoned wagon at the edge of town. "Malone's in there," he whispered. "I'd stake my life on it."

"That is what you are doing," Gray Hawk said. "As well as the lives of El Capitán and the señorita."

The Yaqui didn't have to remind him of that. The Kid knew all too well how much was riding on the actions he would take in the next hour or so. Although the lights of the town made it impossible to see beyond it, he knew that the gray arc of approaching dawn filled more than a quarter of the sky. The breeze held a hint of coolness that could only be found in the hours around dawn.

It was likely that Malone had placed gunmen on top of some of the buildings. They could keep an eye on everything from up there, and they would have a good field of fire for their rifles, as well.

Knowing that, The Kid pointed to a nearby building that didn't have any windows facing them. Gray Hawk nodded. They darted out from behind the wagon and ran to the building, where they slid along the wall to the building's rear corner. Risking a look, The Kid saw a ladder leaning against the rear wall, but none of Malone's men were anywhere in sight. His lips curved in a chilly grin. His hunch seemed to have been confirmed. He motioned for the Yaqui to follow him and went to the ladder.

He didn't try to be quiet as he climbed it. When he got to the top, he stepped over the shallow wall to the building's flat roof. A false front rose above the street to give the illusion of a second story, and as The Kid glanced out from under the pulled-down brim of his hat, he saw two hard cases standing behind that false front, holding rifles. He sauntered toward them, comfortable in the knowledge that he was supposed to be here.

One of the men glanced over a shoulder at him. "It's about time somebody showed up," the man complained. "We was supposed to be relieved half an hour ago."

If Malone had fifty men on his payroll, it was likely that not every one of them knew all the others that well. The Kid needed just enough time to reach the men, and in the shadows atop the roof, he got that. He was within a few steps of them before the second man looked back and said, "Shit, that ain't—"

He didn't get a chance to finish the exclamation. The Kid struck with blinding speed, whipping the butt of his Colt down on the man's head. Even as he buffaloed the hired gun, something flickered past him. The other man staggered and made a gurgling sound. The rifle he'd been holding thudded to the roof. The Kid looked over and saw the man pawing futilely with both hands at the knife embedded in his throat. He finally succeeded in pulling it free, which unleashed a flood of crimson down the front of his shirt.

The Kid grabbed both men—the unconscious one and the dying one—and lowered them to the roof so they wouldn't make a lot of noise when they fell. It was bad enough that they had dropped their rifles. Of course, it wouldn't matter if none of Malone's men were inside the building to hear the thuds.

As The Kid glanced toward the rear of the building, he saw Gray Hawk at the top of the ladder. That had been a hell of a throw, he thought, to plant a knife in the hardcase's throat in poor light. But it didn't surprise him that Gray Hawk had been able to make it. The Kid had a feeling the Yaqui was one of the most dangerous individuals whose trail he had ever crossed. He motioned for Gray Hawk to join him.

From there he could look down the street and across the roofs of the buildings. It was a cross street, but it intersected Main four buildings away, where two more of Malone's men were on top of the roof. They didn't seem to have noticed the commotion Morgan and Gray Hawk had created.

"If we get rid of those two," The Kid whispered, "we can reach the alley that runs behind the Rattler's Den."

Gray Hawk nodded as he retrieved his knife.

"Yes. But we cannot take a chance on this one waking up."

Before The Kid realized what Gray Hawk meant the Yaqui bent over and cut the throat of the man The Kid had knocked out. It was a mighty effective way to make sure the varmint stayed quiet, The Kid thought, and he wasn't going to mourn any gun-wolf who decided to work for a man like Black Terence Malone.

From where he stood The Kid watched the two guards at the corner building. They had their backs to him and Gray Hawk and were looking out at Main Street. The Kid studied the gaps between the buildings, then went back and pulled the ladder up. He laid it across the gap from roof to roof, then glanced at Gray Hawk. The Yaqui nodded approvingly and stepped up to go first, walking across the ladder to the next building with impressive stealth and agility.

The Kid followed. He didn't have any particular fear of heights—those single-story buildings weren't all that tall to begin with—but he *was* aware of the empty air under the ladder as he made the crossing. As soon as he was over, he picked up the ladder and carried it to the next gap between buildings. The false fronts concealed them from any watchers on the roofs across the street, except for the few seconds it took to cross from building to building. They would have to trust to luck that they wouldn't be spotted.

A few minutes later, they stepped onto the roof

of the building at the corner. Their feet crunched a little on the gravel and tarpaper as they came up behind the two sentries. But the men weren't expecting any trouble until dawn, and certainly not any that came from behind them. Though they started to turn around to see what was going on, they didn't have a chance. The Kid slammed his gun into the side of one man's head while Gray Hawk caught the other from behind, clapped his free hand over the gunnie's mouth, and drove the knife into the man's back with his other hand. More blood bubbled onto the roof a moment later as Gray Hawk slashed the throats of both men.

It was brutal business, The Kid thought, but Malone had called the tune for that dance. More importantly, at least four of Malone's men were dead, and it was entirely possible that the other Yaquis were whittling down the odds even more as they slipped into town and took care of any guards they encountered.

Another ladder was in place against the rear wall of the corner building. The Kid and Gray Hawk climbed down it and found themselves in the alley that ran behind the Rattler's Den. They trotted silently along the shadowy passage until they reached the rear of the saloon.

The back door was locked. The Kid looked up and saw a window on the second floor that was open a few inches. They should have brought one of the ladders with them, he thought. The room beyond the open window was dark, and it could be their way in.

He pointed it out to Gray Hawk and whispered, "I can try to boost you up there."

The Yaqui shook his head. "No, I will boost you, as you put it. You are good with a gun, señor, and there may be gun work to do in there."

The Kid couldn't dispute that. He didn't want a gunfight, because the noise would alert the rest of Malone's men scattered through town that something was going on, but it might come to that if he was going to save Diana and her uncle.

"All right," he said. "Let's see if you can get me in there. If I can, I'll come down and unlock that door for you."

Gray Hawk bent down and laced his fingers together to make a step. The Kid put his left foot in it and used his right leg to push himself up as Gray Hawk lifted him. He thrust his arms as far above his head as he could reach and strained to hook his fingers over the sill of the open window.

He caught hold of the sill and hung there for a second with Gray Hawk supporting part of his weight, then gathered his strength and pulled himself up closer to the window. He got an arm all the way over the sill and hooked his elbow on it. The strain in his shoulders was terrific as he used his other hand to push the window up farther.

With his toes finding tiny gaps between the boards of the wall, he pulled himself all the way up so that he could clamber over the window sill and into the room. He sprawled on the floor and wrapped his hand around the butt of the Colt on his hip as he waited to see what was going to happen.

The answer was . . . nothing. The room remained dark and quiet. It was deserted, just as The Kid hoped.

He got to his feet and made his way carefully through the darkness toward the door, or rather, where he hoped the door was. He didn't want to knock anything over and alert his enemies that he was there. When the fingers of his outstretched left hand brushed smooth wood, he slid them down until he found the knob. It turned easily and he eased the door open an inch, no more.

He peered through that narrow gap as light spilled through it. From that angle, he could see a short distance down a dimly lit hallway. It seemed to be empty as well, but he could hear voices coming from somewhere else in the building. One of them was a deep rumble that might belong to Wolfram. That was more evidence, as if The Kid needed it, that Malone had made the Rattler's Den his headquarters in Bristol.

The Kid opened the door farther. He could see that there were other doors along the corridor, but they were all closed. At the end of the hall was the balcony that overlooked the saloon's main room. The Kid stole in to the corridor and made his way toward the balcony.

He stopped when he was still well back where he couldn't be seen easily from below. Taking off his hat, he dropped into a crouch and eased forward, gradually flattening out until he was on his belly. He crawled toward the balcony and paused to look both ways along it before venturing closer to the railing. The balcony was empty.

The Kid suspected that everyone in the building except him was downstairs. Malone would have wanted to have all his prisoners where he could keep an eye on them without much trouble. Keeping his head down, The Kid moved closer to the edge of the balcony.

The long, polished bar came into view. The Kid's heart raced when he saw Sophia Kincaid standing beside it, a worried frown on her beautiful face. She appeared to be all right, and that was a relief to him. Several young women in short, spangled dresses stood at the bar with her. They had to be the girls who worked in the saloon. He didn't see any customers and wondered if Malone had forced them all out at gunpoint when he took over the town. The Kid suspected that if Malone had issued orders for everyone to go back to their homes, most of the folks in Bristol would have obeyed out of fear for their lives.

Farther along the bar, Jefferson Parnell leaned his elbows on the hardwood. He had a drink in front of him and sipped on it from time to time. He looked worried and more than a little frightened, The Kid thought. If the newspaperman was working with Malone, he wouldn't be so scared. The theory that had floated through The Kid's mind earlier about Parnell selling them out to Malone seemed groundless now. But The Kid still had plenty of other questions about Jefferson Parnell.

Those questions would have to wait to be answered. Black Terence himself came into view, strolling over to the bar to stand next to Sophia.

"You might as well relax and have a drink like Parnell there," Malone told her. "This will all be over soon."

"Because everybody from Diamondback will be dead?" Sophia shot back at him with a note of defiance in her voice. "Because you'll be the lord and master of this whole valley?"

"Something like that," Malone admitted with a confident grin.

"You're mighty sure that you're going to win this fight."

"I ought to be. My men outnumber Starbird's this time, and we have the advantage of the high ground. As soon as Rocklin and the others ride into town, they'll be slaughtered like sheep."

"What about Kid Morgan?"

"What about him? He's just one man. I'm not afraid of him. Maybe if we capture him, I'll give him to Wolfram. I think he'd like that . . . wouldn't you, Wolfram?"

An answering growl came from somewhere below the balcony.

"When Wolfram's through with The Kid, how about lettin' Early and me have a crack at him, boss?" That question came from Breck, who was also somewhere underneath the balcony, probably at one of the tables. All of Malone's lieutenants were there.

Malone said, "Sure, if he's still alive, you two can have the pleasure of filling him full of holes, Breck. There's only one man in this valley I care about killing with my own hands." He turned to look to his right. "And you know who that is, don't you, Captain?"

Chapter 28

Owen Starbird didn't respond to Malone's taunting words, but Diana did. "If you hurt him, I'll kill you, Malone!" she blazed. "Somehow, I'll make you pay!"

Malone threw back his head and laughed. "You won't do anything except what I tell you to do, my dear. You're going to be my good, faithful, obedient wife at home on Diamondback—my ranch, Diamondback—while this little morsel," he ran his hand up Sophia's bare arm, "will comfort me whenever I'm in town. Isn't that right?"

"Go to hell," Sophia said through clenched teeth. "Oh, I forgot . . . that's what you're going to turn this valley into, isn't it?"

"If Rattlesnake Valley is hell, then I'm Lucifer himself!" Malone boasted. Again he gave a booming laugh. "This is my kingdom now, and none of you should ever forget it!"

He was loco, The Kid thought. Stark, raving

mad. But the fact that Malone was crazy didn't make him any less dangerous. Malone closed his hand around Sophia's arm and jerked her tightly against him. As he brought his mouth down on hers, she struggled fiercely to get away from him, but she was no match for his huge size and overpowering strength. When he finally broke the kiss, Sophia's hand flashed up and cracked across his face. Malone growled and backhanded her, knocking her to the floor. She cried out in pain as she landed in a huddled heap at Parnell's feet.

"I should have hanged you when I had the chance," Starbird said in the stunned silence.

Malone wheeled around and sneered. "Yes, you should have, Captain," he said, "because you'll never get that opportunity again!"

Breck walked into view, resting his hand on the butt of his revolver. "Gonna be dawn soon," he said as he looked out the saloon's front window. "What if they don't show up, boss?"

"Then we've won without firing a shot," Malone said. "The valley will be ours."

Even with the four killers The Kid knew were all in the saloon—Malone, Wolfram, Breck, and Early—the odds were high against him. He couldn't be sure if more of Malone's men were down there, out of his line of sight, and there was no way he could get downstairs to let Gray Hawk into the building without letting them know he was there. He would have to figure out some way to take all four of them by himself. To do that, he would have to have some sort of distraction . . .

Standing near the front window, Breck suddenly exclaimed, "What the hell!" and clawed at the gun on his hip. Before he could draw the weapon, the window exploded inward at him, sending shards of glass showering all around him. A split second later, the barrel that had just crashed through the window slammed into Breck and knocked him off his feet.

Gray Hawk leaped through the shattered window right behind the barrel he had thrown. The old Yaqui hadn't stayed put. He had taken matters into his own hands, obviously figuring that The Kid couldn't let him into the building but would need help anyway.

As Gray Hawk landed lightly on his feet, he threw his knife. The Kid heard a man cry out in pain and knew the blade had found its target. At the same time, The Kid surged to his feet and drew his Colt. Breck was trying to get up. His face was a mask of blood from dozens of small cuts inflicted by the flying glass. He pawed the crimson away from his eyes with his free hand and swung his gun toward Gray Hawk with the other.

The Kid fired before the gunman could pull the trigger. The bullet smashed into Breck's chest and drove him back down to his knees. The Kid shot him a second time, in the head. Breck flopped backward as the slug bored through his brain and exploded out the back of his skull.

With a roar, Wolfram leaped forward, his arms

going around Gray Hawk in a bear hug. The two men staggered around the room as Gray Hawk tried to break Wolfram's grip.

The Kid wanted to help the Yaqui, but his hands were full at the moment. Redheaded Early came out from under the balcony, gun in hand, and fired up at him. Early's bullets chewed splinters from the railing as The Kid ducked back to avoid them.

"You son of a bitch!" Early howled. "You killed Breck!"

The Kid ran for the stairs. He had to get down there. From the corner of his eye he had seen Malone jerk Sophia in front of him to serve as a human shield as the bullets began to fly. More of Early's slugs whistled through the air in front of The Kid, however, forcing him to throw on the brakes short of the staircase.

Well, hell, The Kid thought. He would just have to get down some other way.

He lunged toward the balcony railing, put his left hand on it, and vaulted over it. He hoped it wasn't as crazy a move as it appeared to be, as he found himself falling through the air.

Luck cooperated with him. Early had to hold his fire as The Kid dropped straight toward Wolfram and Gray Hawk. He landed on Wolfram's back with a strong enough impact to knock the big bruiser away from the Yaqui. All three men fell against a felt-covered table that collapsed under their weight. They sprawled on the floor in a welter of debris and a tangle of arms and legs.

The Kid fought his way free of that confusion first and came up on his knees. A gun roared and a slug sizzled past his ear. He spotted Early over the barrel of his gun and pulled the trigger. Early doubled over and stumbled back a step as The Kid's lead punched hotly into his guts.

Wolfram swung an arm like the trunk of a young tree and slammed it into the side of The Kid's head. The blow sent him sliding across the sawdust-littered floor of the saloon.

He managed to hang on to his gun. As bullets thudded into the planks beside him, he rolled over and drilled the hard case who was firing at him. The Kid's bullets turned the man's face into a crimson smear.

"Kid, look out!" Diana screamed.

What felt like a mountain fell on The Kid. The crushing weight drove all the air from his lungs and made red lightning flash before his eyes. He knew that Wolfram was on top of him, but before he could squirm away, Wolfram's arm looped around his neck from behind and tightened on his throat. The Kid felt his spine stretching and bending as Wolfram dug a knee into the small of his back and hauled upward with the arm around his neck, reversing the positions they had been in during the climax of their first battle.

The Kid couldn't see anything except what was right in front of him. Diana and Owen Starbird sat at one of the tables. Diana was tied hand and foot and lashed to the chair to keep her from getting away, but Starbird was free. He didn't have his crutches, though, so there was nothing he could do except sit there.

Or was there? The Kid was in too much pain and on the verge of blacking out from lack of air to really comprehend what was going on at first, but then he realized that Starbird was trying to stand up. The captain's hands were on the table, and the muscles of his arms and shoulders and neck stood out as he strained to lift himself onto his legs. His face flushed red from the exertion. He rose higher and higher in his chair until he was balanced precariously on those wasted legs.

"My God," Diana breathed. "Uncle Owen . . ."

Starbird was standing, one hand on the table, the other on the back of the chair where he had been sitting. With a look of intense determination on his face, he tried to take a step toward The Kid and Wolfram.

He fell flat on his face.

Diana cried out in mingled disappointment and pity.

But Starbird wasn't through. His arms still worked just fine. He got his hands underneath him and levered himself forward, lifting his torso from the floor and dragging his legs behind him. Wolfram might have seen him coming, but he didn't look up from the task of choking The Kid to death, which he was carrying out with fiendish glee.

The Kid saw Starbird's struggle to help him, and encouraged the man on with his eyes.

When Starbird was close enough, he swung a fist and crashed it against the side of Wolfram's head. The former pirate grunted in pain and surprise, and his grip on The Kid loosened just enough. The Kid drove an elbow back into Wolfram's midsection with as much force as he could muster. At the same time, he twisted his body, and Wolfram's arm came loose from around his neck. The Kid dragged air gratefully through his tortured throat.

As The Kid rolled away, Starbird smashed punch after punch into Wolfram's face. Years of relying on his arms to get him around, either on crutches or in the wheelchair, had given him incredible strength. Then, while Wolfram was stunned, Starbird fastened both hands on the man's neck and began to squeeze.

Wolfram bucked and flailed, but he couldn't dislodge Starbird's grip. The two men rolled across the floor, locked in their deadly struggle.

A few yards away, The Kid surged to his feet. He realized that he had dropped his gun during the fight with Wolfram. He looked for it as a bullet whipped past his ear. A woman screamed.

The Kid whirled and saw Black Terence Malone backing toward the batwinged entrance to the saloon. He still had Sophia in front of him, holding her there with one arm while he used his other hand to aim his gun at The Kid. Sophia was putting up such a fight he figured she had thrown off Malone's aim and caused his first shot to miss. The

Kid watched as she leaned over and sunk her teeth into Malone's arm, causing him to jerk around and howl in pain.

Malone hit Sophia with the gun in his hand. It was a brutal blow to the head that made her go limp. As Malone let go of her and she slumped to the floor, The Kid spotted his gun lying a few feet away and dived for it. Malone threw a shot at him, but the bullet went over The Kid's head. His fingers closed on the gun butt and he scooped up the Colt, but as he tilted the barrel toward Malone and pulled the trigger, the pirate flung himself through the batwings, out of the saloon. The Kid's bullet knocked a slat out of one of the swinging doors.

The Kid was aware that a lot of gunfire was coming from outside the Rattler's Den. Sam Rocklin and the men from Diamondback had arrived, and, along with Gray Hawk's Yaqui brethren, they were engaged in pitched battle with Malone's forces. The Kid hoped that the innocent citizens of Bristol would keep their heads down as long as the bullets were flying. In the larger picture, though, no one in Rattlesnake Valley would ever be safe until the threat of Black Terence Malone had been dealt with. Some risks had to be run if people were going to be free.

After all, the only people who were truly safe . . . were the ones who were already dead. They could never be hurt again.

Sophia was hurt, though. Blood welled from the gash in her forehead that the blow from Malone's gun had opened up. The Kid hurried to her side and knelt to lift her and cradle her head on his thigh. Her eyelids fluttered, then stayed open. She gazed up at him with no recognition at first, then said weakly, "Kid?"

"That's right," he told her. "How bad are you hurt?"

"I . . . I don't know. My head hurts like blazes."

The Kid hoped that she had just been knocked out for a few moments and that Malone's craven blow hadn't done any real damage.

Elsewhere in the saloon, Gray Hawk had managed to climb to his feet. He was moving stiffly, which told The Kid that he was in pain. The old Yaqui might have some cracked ribs from that bear hug Wolfram had caught him in.

As for Wolfram, the massive former pirate lay motionless on his back, his tongue and eyeballs protruding slightly in death. Owen Starbird was still sprawled on top of him with fingers locked around Wolfram's throat. Starbird looked like he had passed out.

Gray Hawk bent and pulled his knife from the chest of one of Malone's gunmen. He shuffled over to the table where a wide-eyed Diana still sat, lashed to the chair. "I will cut you loose, señorita," the Yaqui said.

"Thanks, Gray Hawk," she said. She looked over at The Kid and asked, "Where did Malone go?"

The Kid shook his head as he gently pushed back some strands of rich brown hair that had fallen over

Sophia's eyes. "I don't know, but he must've wound up in the middle of that battle going on out there. He may be dead now, for all I know."

"Whatever happens to him, it won't be as bad as he deserves," Diana said as Gray Hawk's knife began severing the cords that bound her to the chair and held her wrists and ankles tightly together. "The man was insane!"

The Kid nodded. "Eighteen years in prison helped make him that way, but my guess is that he was evil to start with." He looked around the room, which stank of gunsmoke, and asked, "What happened to Parnell?"

"He's gone," Diana said. "I didn't see him leave. He must have slipped out when all the shooting and fighting started."

Sophia brought The Kid's attention back to her by saying, "Kid, I-I think I could use a drink. As nice as it is lying here with you holding me, I need to stand up."

"Sure," he said. "Put your arms around my neck."

She lifted her arms and draped them around his neck as he got a good grip on her. Then he straightened to his feet and brought her up with him.

Gray Hawk had cut Diana loose. She stood as well and rubbed her wrists to get the feeling back into her hands. Her steps were unsteady as she came toward The Kid and Sophia. All of them arrived at the bar at just about the same time, with

The Kid standing between the two lovely young women.

"What happened to your bartenders and all your customers when Malone came in and took over the place?" The Kid asked Sophia.

"He told them to get out. He had his men round everybody up and ordered them to get in their houses and stay there until he told them to come out again. Nobody wanted to cross him, so they did like he said."

The Kid nodded. "That's what I figured. Will you ladies be all right for a minute while Gray Hawk and I check on Captain Starbird?"

"Sure," Sophia said. She reached over and snagged a bottle someone had left on the bar. "You want a drink, Diana?"

"Don't mind if I do," Diana said. She took the bottle from Sophia, lifted it to her lips, and downed a healthy slug of the whiskey. Then she handed it back to Sophia, who swallowed about half of the amber liquid that was left.

The Kid was glad to see that the two of them seemed to have called a truce in their ongoing dislike for each other. He and Gray Hawk went over to Starbird and lifted the man off Wolfram's corpse. They carried him back to the chair where he had been sitting earlier and lowered him into it. Starbird was coming around. He shook his head from side to side and muttered incoherently.

"It must have taken every bit of strength he had to choke the life out of that monster," The Kid said.

Gray Hawk nodded. "Truly, the señor is a brave, gallant man."

The Kid couldn't argue with that. Owen Starbird had saved his life. Wolfram would have broken The Kid's back in another minute or two.

The gunfire outside had died away to an occasional sporadic shot. The Kid hoped that meant the battle was over—and that the men from Diamondback had won. He didn't know for sure, so he quickly thumbed fresh cartridges from his belt into his Colt to replace the ones he had fired, then stepped to the batwings to look outside. The sun was up, but it was still low in the eastern sky, filling the streets of Bristol with rosy light.

That light didn't soften the grimness of the sight that met The Kid's eyes. Bodies were sprawled in the street and along the boardwalks. He saw Yaquis, he saw punchers he recognized from Diamondback, he saw hardbitten strangers who had to be some of Malone's bunch of killers. The toll taken by this battle was a heavy one.

A flurry of shots came from somewhere down the street. Men shouted and cursed. The Kid stepped on the boardwalk and saw Sam Rocklin, along with some of the punchers and Gray Hawk's Yaquis, running toward the saloon, firing over their shoulders at masked, duster-clad men who pursued them on horseback.

What the hell?

The Kid shouted, "Sam! In here!", and the fleeing men veered toward the saloon. The Kid waved

them on and fired his Colt over their heads at the
riders. "We'll fort up inside!"

Rocklin and the others swarmed into the saloon.
The Kid dove through the batwings after them as
bullets punched holes in the doors and shattered
the remaining glass in the windows.

"Down!" The Kid bellowed. "Everybody down!"

He heard Sophia and Diana scream as he flattened out in scattered glass beneath one of the windows. Rocklin was beside him. They began firing
at the riders, and some of the others were already
at the other window, peppering the masked men on
horseback as well. The riders wheeled their mounts
and withdrew, but The Kid had a hunch they
weren't giving up. They were just regrouping for
another attack on the saloon.

"Sam, what in blazes is going on here?" The Kid
asked as a lull fell over the street. He took advantage of it to reload again.

"Beats the hell outta me, Kid!" the foreman
replied. "I thought we just about had Malone's
bunch wiped out, when all of a sudden that other
gang of gunnies came a-swarmin' down on us from
outside of town. I don't know where they came
from or who they are!"

Neither did The Kid, but he knew one thing as
he lifted his head enough to glance out the broken
window.

"Here they come again!" he yelled.

Chapter 29

The Kid twisted his head around to call over his shoulder, "Some of you get upstairs and cover those windows! The rest take the back! Don't let any of that bunch get inside that way! A couple of you men grab Captain Starbird and help him behind the bar. Diana, you and Sophia stay with your uncle and keep your heads down!"

The Diamondback hands and the Yaquis scattered to follow The Kid's orders. None too soon, because guns began to bang again and bullets flew through the empty spaces where the windows had been busted out.

Staying low, The Kid and Rocklin and the men at the other window returned the fire. The mysterious riders swept past, pouring lead into the saloon as they galloped by, then wheeled their horses around for another pass.

Each time, though, The Kid was gratified to see a couple of them tumble from their saddles.

The problem was that this new and unexpected enemy numbered at least forty, and The Kid doubted if the combined forces of the defenders inside the saloon added up to more than thirty. They had the advantage of being able to fort up in there, but at the same time, they were pinned down, and it was only a matter of time before the masked gunmen shot the building to pieces.

That didn't take into account the possibility that they might decide to start a fire and burn the defenders out.

The riders withdrew again. The Kid guessed they were trying to decide the most effective way of dealing with the holdouts in the saloon. He risked a look and saw them down at the end of the street, gathered in a knot. As The Kid studied them, his eyes narrowed as he concentrated on one particular mounted figure. The man was tall and broad-shouldered, and even though he had a bandanna drawn up over the lower half of his face, there was something familiar about him. When The Kid saw the early morning sunlight reflect off something under the broad brim of the man's hat, everything that had been bothering him for the past few days fell into place.

He stood up.

"Kid, what are you doin'?" Rocklin said. "Better get down. That bunch could start shootin' again."

"I know what I'm doing, Sam," The Kid said. Holding his gun tightly, he went to the batwings and pushed one of them out a little. He raised his voice and shouted, "Parnell! Jefferson Parnell!"

At the end of the street, the masked figure he'd been studying stiffened in the saddle and then turned to look toward The Kid. Parnell's eyesight was bad enough that he had to wear his spectacles, even when he pulled on the duster and mask of a mysterious marauder.

"Let's talk this over, Parnell!" The Kid called. "Maybe everybody doesn't have to die!"

Behind the bar, Sophia's head popped up. "Parnell?" she repeated in amazement. "The newspaperman?"

Without taking his eyes off the enemy, The Kid said, "I've got a hunch he isn't a real newspaperman. Or if he is, publishing a paper isn't why he's here in Rattlesnake Valley."

Parnell separated himself from the rest of the gunmen and rode slowly toward the saloon. He said something sharply over his shoulder to the others, maybe ordering them to stay put while he parleyed with The Kid. Parnell brought his horse to a halt in front of the saloon and said, "Step out here where we can see each other while we talk, Morgan."

"I'm not sure that's a good idea," The Kid said. "You could have a man drawing a bead on me as soon as I come out onto the boardwalk."

"I probably have a dozen or more guns trained on me right now," Parnell snapped. "I think it's only fair that you have to worry about that, too."

Rocklin whispered, "Don't do it, Kid," and when he glanced back he saw Diana and Sophia peering over the bar, both of them shaking their heads.

But he said, "All right, Parnell. If you or your men try any tricks, though, I can guarantee you'll never make it back up the street alive."

"No tricks," Parnell promised. "I just want to indulge my curiosity and find out how much you know."

"I know enough," The Kid said as he pushed the batwings aside and stepped onto the boardwalk. "I know that the river George Starbird uncovered is one of the best sources of water between San Antonio and El Paso. I also know that if somebody were to use dynamite and blast that pass closed in the mountains, then build a dam across the opening in the hills at the other end of the valley, within a year or two you'd have a mighty fine reservoir right here. The town and all the ranches would be covered up, of course, but there would be millions of gallons of water that could make a man rich. This is West Texas, after all. Water is money."

Parnell tugged his bandanna down, revealing the angry glare on his face. "How did you figure that out?" he demanded.

"I've had a few engineering courses in my time," The Kid said without elaborating. "As soon as I saw the layout of the valley, I knew there was something unusual about it. It just took me a few days to figure out that it's shaped to be a natural reservoir. All anybody would have to do is close off those two openings. That would dam up the river. I don't know how you found out about it, but you saw the potential. And when you came here to see if you could exploit it, you found a tailor-made situation to get what you wanted. Malone was crazy for revenge on Captain Starbird. All you had to do was poke both sides a little to make it happen faster. You brought in gunmen and had them hide out in the hills. They're the ones who rustled Diamondback stock and took potshots at Diamondback hands. You wanted Starbird so mad and worried that he'd strike first, then he and Malone and all their men could wipe each other out, leaving the valley as easy pickings for you to take over." The Kid shook his head. "Malone didn't cooperate, even though he had no idea what you were doing. You sent Diamondback over to Trident last night for the final showdown, but Malone and his men weren't there. They were at Diamondback, grabbing Starbird and his niece to use as hostages to force a showdown of *their* choosing, here in town. Just pure bad luck and bad timing, Parnell, or things might have played out the way you wanted."

It was a long speech, and The Kid was a little hoarse by the time he finished it. He had been putting the theory together in his head as he spoke, and when he saw how neatly it all fit together, he was convinced it was true.

Parnell confirmed that by saying, "You're a

smart bastard, Morgan, but what good is it going to do you? You and your friends are trapped here."

"What are you going to do?" asked The Kid. "Wipe out the whole town, once you've finished us off?"

Parnell smiled, and the cold malice in the expression made a chill go up and down The Kid's spine. "That's exactly what I'm going to do," Parnell said. "I'm tired of waiting. There's going to be a great tragedy here today, Morgan. The citizens of Bristol are going to be killed in the crossfire of a big battle between Diamondback and Trident, and the town is going to be set on fire and burned to the ground. There won't be anything left here to save or rebuild. Malone has no heirs, and neither do Starbird and his niece. Their ranches will go to the state, and the men who are backing me will help me swoop in and gather them up. The same holds true for the little ranchers. All of them can be bought out cheaply. You see, Morgan, nothing can stop progress. Building a reservoir here is for the greater good."

"And it'll make you a mighty rich man in the process."

Parnell shrugged. "That's beside the point, isn't it?"

"And all you have to do is murder a couple hundred people."

"I told you," Parnell snapped, "it's for the greater good."

"You can tell yourself that all you want, mister.

You're still a murdering outlaw as far as I'm concerned."

"Then it's a good thing there's nothing you can do to stop me," Parnell said, smiling again.

"Now, you see, that's where you're wrong," The Kid said.

His gun came up in a blur of speed and he shot Jefferson Parnell right smack between the eyes.

Parnell fell backward off his horse before he even had a chance to look surprised. By the time his body thudded to the ground, The Kid had whirled around and dived back through the batwings. Shots roared out from the men down the street, but they were too late. The bullets chewed up the boardwalk and smacked into the saloon's front wall.

As The Kid scrambled back over to the window, Rocklin asked, "Was all that crazy story about turnin' the valley into a lake true?"

"You heard Parnell," The Kid said. "He admitted it."

Rocklin shook his head. "Plumb loco, if you ask me." He nodded toward the street. "You reckon the rest of his bunch will give it up now that he's dead?"

The sound of shots rose to a veritable barrage as Parnell's men continued firing.

"I kind of doubt it," The Kid said in answer to Rocklin's question. "Some of those gunmen are bound to know what was at stake here. They'll try to take advantage of Parnell's death and grab the prize for themselves."

"Yeah, and here they come to do some grabbin' now!" Rocklin yelled as the thunder of hoofbeats filled the air outside the saloon, along with the gunshots.

For the next few minutes, the action was fast and furious inside the saloon, as well as out in the street. The air was filled with the stink of powder-smoke, the roar of shots, and the whistle and whine of hot lead. Crouched at the window, The Kid emptied his Colt, reloaded, and emptied the gun again. More of Parnell's hired killers fell to the defenders' bullets, but some of the men inside the saloon went down, too, most of them just wounded but a few mortally injured.

Then the attackers swung around and galloped off down the street again. Their direct assault on the Rattler's Den had failed, but The Kid had no doubt that they would be back.

"See to the wounded," he ordered as he reloaded again. He was running low on fresh cartridges, and he suspected that many of the other defenders were, too. A couple of more attacks like that and the men in the saloon would be out of ammunition.

"Morgan!" Owen Starbird called from behind the bar. The Kid went over to see what he wanted. Starbird looked up at him and said, "This is not a sustainable position, Morgan. Those bloody bastards will exhaust our ammunition with continuing attacks and then overrun us when we can no longer fight back."

The Kid nodded. "I know, Captain. You have any ideas how we can turn the tables on them?"

"Indeed. We need to close quarters with them. Our fire will be most effective that way."

"You mean let them in here?" The Kid asked with a frown.

"It's the only way," Starbird said. "Our forces are still relatively even with theirs, are they not?"

"I reckon they outnumber us by a few."

"But not all that many. And they have no way of knowing exactly how many of us are left. I suggest that most of us withdraw to the second floor, leaving a few men down here to put up only a token resistance the next time they attack, and then fire down on them when they rush in here thinking that they've won."

The Kid thought about it for a second, then nodded. "That might work. But if it doesn't, we're all dead."

"If the situation continues as it is, we shall all die anyway."

The Kid couldn't argue with that. He said, "All right. We'll try to draw them in and have the showdown while we've still got some bullets."

Quickly, he passed the word to everyone else. "We'll leave three men down here to put up a fight," he explained. "Everybody else will be upstairs, and when those varmints come rushing in to finish us off, let them have it. Just hold your fire until most of them are inside."

"I'm one of the three who'll stay down here," Rocklin declared without hesitation.

"And I'm another," Starbird said.

Diana shook her head. "Uncle Owen, you know that's not possible. Some of the men will take you upstairs—"

"Blast it, girl!" Starbird reached up, grasped the top of the bar, and started pulling himself to his feet. "I've put up with you giving me orders because I know you think it's best, but no longer! Some of you lads give me a hand here. Put me in a chair by the window, and I can shoot at those bounders just fine!"

"Uncle Owen—" Diana began stubbornly, but The Kid stopped her with a hand on her arm.

"It's his decision," The Kid said. He nodded to Starbird. "I know I'd be proud to have you fighting at my side, Captain."

"So you'll be the third man, huh? Can't say as I'm surprised." Starbird looked around, then roared in a voice that must have carried easily from one end of HMS *Scorpion*'s deck to the other, "Well? Someone give me a hand here!"

Diana frowned at The Kid as several of the punchers from Diamondback helped Starbird get into position by one of the shattered front windows. A man picked up an overturned chair, set it upright, and the others lowered Starbird onto it. Another man handed him a pair of pistols.

"This is splendid!" Starbird said as he hefted the guns. "Just splendid!"

"He had better come through this alive," Diana warned The Kid in a low voice.

"There's no guarantee any of us will," The Kid told her. "Do your part. Grab a gun and get ready to cut down some of those gunmen when they come rushing in here."

She jerked her head in a nod. "Damn right I will."

Once they had decided on the plan, it didn't take long to put it into action. The Kid and Rocklin took their places at the other window while all the rest of the defenders hurried upstairs. The Kid spotted Sophia carrying a double-barreled shotgun she took from under the bar. He caught her eye and asked, "Can you use that greener?"

"You just hide and watch," she said with a determined nod. The blood from the cut on her forehead had dried in a streak down her face, but even with that savage decoration, she still managed to look lovely.

It was a good thing everyone moved as quickly as they did, because no sooner were the other defenders upstairs than Rocklin called out, "Get ready! Yonder they come again!"

"Space your shots out like you're trying to conserve bullets," The Kid told him and Starbird.

That was actually what they were trying to do, he thought. They had to defeat Parnell's men right there in the saloon in the next few minutes, or not at all. Victory or death . . . that sure boiled things right down to the nub.

Hoofbeats thundered and guns began to roar. The Kid, Rocklin, and Starbird returned the fire as slugs chipped away at the saloon's walls. The Kid squeezed off a couple of deliberately spaced shots and saw one of the attackers go backwards out of the saddle. Despite that, he sensed a new urgency on the part of the masked killers. They sensed victory, and like sharks smelling blood in the water, they were ready to swarm.

"Watch out, Kid!" Rocklin yelled as one of the men leaped his horse onto the porch and sent the animal charging right through the space where the big window had been. The Kid and Rocklin had to fling themselves to right and left to keep from being trampled.

More riders jumped on the porch, forcing their mounts through the windows and past the batwings. Others dismounted and charged in on foot. In a matter of seconds, the saloon's main room was crowded with masked, duster-clad gunmen.

"Let 'em have it!" The Kid bellowed. The Colt bucked in his hand as he shot another of the killers out of the saddle.

The noise from dozens of pistols, rifles, and shotguns going off at once in the saloon was deafening. The Kid staggered as it seemed like the sound itself was going to pound him off his feet. He stayed upright and drilled another gunman. From the corner of his eye, he saw that Sam Rocklin had fought his way to Starbird's side. The foreman had lifted Starbird out of the chair and stood with his left arm around him, holding Starbird up as both of them continued firing into the mass of attackers.

It was utter, bloody chaos in the Rattler's Den. Horses screamed as blood spurted from the wounds they suffered. Men fell to the floor and were trampled into ugly shapes that hardly looked human. Some of the defenders were mortally wounded and toppled from the balcony, vanishing into the melee. The place was a hornet's nest of blood and death and flying lead.

The hammer of The Kid's Colt clicked on an empty chamber. He reached up, grabbed a long coat, and hauled the man out of the saddle. The Kid's gun slammed into the man's head and shattered bone. He shoved the dying gun-wolf aside and stumbled over to join Starbird and Rocklin. He saw blood on the clothes of both men, but they were still upright, still fighting. The Kid scooped a pair of fallen revolvers from the floor as he joined them, and all three men fired at once. Two of the raiders went down, shredded into crimson ruin by the hail of bullets.

Then, suddenly, an eerie silence struck the saloon like the blow of a fist. The Kid stood there, breathing heavily, gunsmoke stinging his nose and mouth and eyes, as he looked around and saw that all the attackers were down. Some of them were only wounded, but their moans ceased abruptly as the Yaquis dropped lithely among them from the balcony and knives flashed. Diana and Sophia both turned away from the grisly sight.

"Is . . . is it over?" Rocklin asked.

"Looks like it," The Kid said. "I reckon the town's safe now, and so is the rest of the valley. It won't be underwater after all." He glanced at Starbird. "Unless that's what you want, Captain. This *would* make a good reservoir."

"That's something to think about on another day," Starbird replied. "Sam, will you help me sit down?"

"Sure, Cap'n." Rocklin carefully lowered his employer back onto the chair.

Diana rushed down the stairs, followed by Sophia. Diana threw her arms around her uncle, saying, "Are you all right? You're bleeding!"

"Minor injuries only, I assure you, my dear," Starbird told her. "Nothing to be alarmed about."

Sophia looked up at The Kid. "How about you, Kid?"

"I'm fine," he said with a smile. "I don't think I even got nicked."

"How in the world did you manage that?"

"Just lucky, I guess," Kid Morgan said.

She put a hand on his arm, and the message in her green eyes was clear. He could be even luckier . . . if he wanted.

But though he returned the smile she gave him, he turned away. There was still one more thing he had to do.

He wanted to make sure that Black Terence Malone was dead.

Chapter 30

The former pirate's body was nowhere to be found in the welter of corpses littering the streets and boardwalks of Bristol.

Owen Starbird insisted that it was nothing to worry about, that Malone was no threat anymore. His men were dead and his hold on the valley had been broken. Despite that, The Kid could tell that Starbird was concerned and would have felt better if Malone's body had been among the dead.

The Kid felt exactly the same way.

Of course, it was possible that Malone had been wounded and had slunk off somewhere to die. If that was the case, they might find his body later, outside of town. Until then, The Kid was going to be watchful, but that was nothing new. Being careful and alert was the way he stayed alive.

The citizens of Bristol emerged from their hiding places and helped clean up the town. Close to a hundred bodies were carried to the undertaker's and stacked behind the building like cordwood. Guards were posted to keep scavengers away from the corpses, and teams of gravediggers would work around the clock to get all the dead men into the ground. Bristol's cemetery was going to be a mighty busy place for the next couple of days. In fact, there was a bustling air of renewed energy about the whole town now that it was out from under Malone's thumb.

That realization left a slightly bitter taste in The Kid's mouth. Other people had done the hard, bloody work of securing freedom once again, and the citizens who had cowered and carped would reap the benefits.

But he supposed that was the way it had always been.

He rode away from the settlement with Diana, Starbird, Rocklin, and the survivors from Diamondback. He didn't figure he would ever return, unless it was briefly to replenish his supplies before he left Rattlesnake Valley.

Gray Hawk and the Yaquis who had lived through the fight had already vanished, taking their dead and wounded with them. That was their way, The Kid supposed. Gray Hawk would probably return to his cave in the mountains, and the other Yaquis would go back wherever they had come from.

It was midafternoon when the group rode up to Diamondback headquarters. The Kid and Rocklin were in the lead, followed by the buggy that

Sophia Kincaid had loaned to Diana and Starbird. The rest of the punchers followed. As the riders reined in, the screen door of the big house opened, and Carmelita stepped out onto the porch, saying, "Señor?"

The Kid stiffened as he spotted the man behind her. Terence Malone stood there, one arm around Carmelita's stout figure while his other hand held a sword to her throat.

"You like to hide behind women, don't you, Malone?" The Kid drawled, forcing himself to stay calm and not show the surprise and anger he felt. He'd had a hunch that Malone would try something if he'd survived the battle in town, but The Kid hadn't expected him to strike quite so soon.

"Unhand that wonderful woman, you . . . you bounder!" Starbird cried as he leaned forward on the buggy seat. "Lads! Your weapons!"

The Kid held up his left hand and called sharply, "Hold your fire!" The cowboys couldn't shoot Malone without hitting Carmelita, too. Not even someone as fast and accurate as he was could make a shot like that. It would take perfect aim.

"Everybody get out of here!" Malone yelled, his voice shaking with fury. "Everybody but Starbird! We're gonna settle this like we should have nearly twenty years ago, man to man!"

"I'll fight you, you scoundrel!" Starbird said. "Any way you'd like, fists, guns, knives . . ."

"Swords." Malone moved a foot behind him, used his toe to hook something he had placed there earlier, and kicked another sword into view, sending it sliding across the porch to clatter down the steps. "I been savin' 'em for this day. Now everybody else clear out, or this fat cow dies!"

Starbird sputtered for a second in his outrage, then said, "How dare you talk about Carmelita like that? She's one of the finest women I've ever known! If you harm her, I swear I'll see to it that you suffer the torments of the damned, Malone!"

The pirate laughed. "Sounds like you've gone soft on her. A stiff-necked bastard like you? I wouldn't have thought it, Captain."

"Just let her go," Starbird said. "Your grudge is against me, not her or anyone else here. Just me."

Malone nodded. "That's why I want to settle this, just the two of us."

Diana said, "We're not going anywhere, Malone. You let Carmelita go right now, or . . . or . . ."

"Or what?" Malone asked with a sneer. "What can you do?"

Starbird said, "He's right. I'm the only one who can do anything, and so I shall. Sam!"

"Yeah, Cap'n?" Rocklin growled.

"Take the men and leave."

"You can't mean that, boss—"

"I most certainly do," Starbird snapped. "That's an order, Sam. I'll fight this battle myself. It was always going to come down to this, and I think I knew that, whether I wanted to acknowledge it or not."

"But Uncle Owen, you can't," Diana protested. "You can't get around—"

"I can use my wheelchair. Will you agree to that, Malone?"

A grin creased Malone's face. "Sure. I'd like to see that, in fact."

Diana shook her head and said to her uncle, "He'll still cut you to pieces!"

"As long as Carmelita and the rest of you are safe, that's all I care about, my dear. Now, go with Sam and the rest of the men." Starbird looked intently at his niece. "If you love me, you'll do as I ask. This is my fight."

"Hold on a minute," The Kid said.

Malone glared at him. "What do you want, Morgan?"

"It sounds to me like you're challenging Captain Starbird to a duel. I'd say that because of his medical condition, he has a right to have a proxy act on his behalf."

"A proxy!" The exclamation startled out of Malone. "What the hell are you talkin' about?"

The Kid nodded toward the sword lying in the dust at the foot of the steps. "I'll fight you in the captain's place."

"Haw!" Malone burst out scornfully. "I know what you're tryin' to do, gunfighter. If I agree to that, you'll just shoot me as soon as you get the chance!"

The Kid shook his head and started to unbuckle his gunbelt. "No. I'm talking about a fair fight, you and me with those swords. No guns." He took the gunbelt off, coiled it, and held it out to Rocklin. "Hang on to this for me, would you, Sam?"

Rocklin hesitated, then took the Colt. "You sure about this, Kid?"

"Morgan, this won't do at all," Starbird said. "Malone's an expert with a blade. At least, he was during his buccaneering days, and I doubt if he's lost much skill."

"Not a whit," Malone said with a grin. "You know, I've got a grudge against you, too, Morgan, so I sort of like this idea. I'll gut you, then Starbird."

The Kid nodded. "We have an agreement, then. Let the woman go."

"Not on your life. She stays right where she is until all the rest are gone and it's just you, me, and Starbird."

"Diana, I insist you leave with Sam and the others," Starbird told his niece. "Please go now."

She looked a little stunned by everything that was happening as she said, "But . . . but—"

"Go on, Diana," The Kid urged her. "It's the only way." He swung down from the buckskin's back, took off his coat, and put it and his hat on the saddle. Then he stepped forward to pick up the sword. He swung it back and forth a couple of times, awkwardly, as he gauged the weight and balance of the weapon.

"Go . . . please," Starbird whispered to Diana.

She let out a tortured cry and started to sob, but

when Rocklin brought his horse over beside the buggy and took his foot out of the stirrup on that side, Diana used it to swing up behind him. Rocklin looked at Starbird and asked, "You're sure, Cap'n?"

"Positive." Starbird smiled. "Look after things if it becomes necessary, will you, Sam?"

"Bet a hat on it," Rocklin replied in a voice choked with emotion. Then he waved a hand at the other punchers and said, "Come on, boys. We'll ride a mile or so back up the trail."

They trotted off, leaving Starbird in the buggy, Malone and Carmelita on the porch, and The Kid standing there facing the former pirate and his hostage. Malone didn't release Carmelita as he waited for the dust from the horses to travel a good distance away from the house.

Starbird said, "You know that the lads won't let you leave here alive, Malone."

"I don't give a damn about that," Malone said with a harsh laugh. "I just want you dead, Starbird. You and that troublemaking young fool." He sneered at The Kid. "You should have turned around and ridden away the first day you saw my skull and crossbones, Morgan."

"That wasn't meant to be," The Kid said quietly.

"No, but your death was." Malone suddenly gave Carmelita a hard shove that sent her staggering along the porch. He leaped down the steps, swinging the sword as he yelled, "Have at you!"

Sunlight flashed on The Kid's blade as it leaped

up to block Malone's blow. Metal rang against metal. The impact of the collision drove The Kid back a step. Malone chopped at him again and forced him to continue giving ground.

Malone changed tactics abruptly, switching from raw power to finesse. The tip of his blade darted at The Kid's legs. The Kid twisted aside, but not before the sword ripped through his trousers and left a shallow gash in his thigh. The wound was painful but didn't come close to disabling him. He parried Malone's follow-up thrust and saw the sudden flash of surprise in the pirate's eyes. Malone had thought he had him, that the fight was over almost before it started.

The Kid counterattacked.

Steel rang against steel again and again as the two men plunged back and forth across the yard in front of the ranch house. The Kid nicked Malone in the side, causing a red bloodstain to blossom on Malone's shirt. Neither man seemed able to strike a fatal blow. They were evenly matched.

Then one of The Kid's feet slipped just a little . . . but it was enough to make him lose his balance and Malone's blade slipped past his. The thrust was an awkward one, and as The Kid tried to twist aside from it, the flat of Malone's blade struck him hard on the side of the head, just above his left ear. The blow drove him off his feet and sent him rolling toward the porch.

The pounding of his heartbeat and the rushing of blood in his head filled his ears, but even so, he heard the sudden rattling buzz from somewhere nearby. As he came to a stop on his hands and knees, he saw the rattlesnake with the diamond-shaped markings on its scaly skin coiled next to the porch, only a couple of feet away from him. He flung himself desperately to the side as the rattler struck.

Malone had been coming in from behind The Kid, sword raised for a killing stroke. Instead, Malone screamed as the striking snake missed The Kid and sank its fangs into Malone's thigh. Malone's blade flashed down and cut the snake in two, but it clung stubbornly to his flesh until he reached down and tore it free. As he threw it aside in revulsion, he panted and laughed.

"I can feel the poison pumpin' through my veins," he said, "but I'll send you and Starbird to hell before me, Morgan!"

He lunged at The Kid once again, attacking with the fierce desperation of knowing that he had only a few minutes before the snake's venom killed him.

The Kid might have been able to hold him off that long and let the rattler's bite do the work for him. Instead, The Kid's blade flashed back and forth, parrying the blows too swiftly for the eye to follow, and then with a sudden lunge he buried the cold steel in Black Terence Malone's chest with such force that the sword went all the way through Malone's body and several inches ripped out through his back.

Malone dropped his sword and swayed, his eyes widening in shock. "How . . . how . . . you're a . . . gunfighter . . ."

The Kid leaned closer to him and said quietly, "Fencing champion, back in my university days. We used to practice with swords, to make the foils seem even lighter."

He let go of the sword. Malone gave out with a groan and toppled forward. He spasmed a couple of times and then didn't move again.

The Kid turned toward the buggy where Starbird sat watching him with amazement. Carmelita stood beside the vehicle, holding Starbird's hand. The Kid reached for the buckskin's reins and said, "Now it's over, Captain. I'd better go let Diana and Sam know that they can come back."

"My God, Morgan!" Starbird burst out. "Where did you learn to handle a blade like that?"

"In another life," Kid Morgan replied with the faintest of smiles.

That evening, The Kid dismounted in front of the Rattler's Den, limping just a little from the wound on his thigh. As he had ridden into town, he was struck by how quickly things had gotten back to a semblance of normalcy in Bristol, although the undertaker and his helpers would certainly be burning the midnight oil. Folks were moving around, and talk and laughter came from inside the saloon as he stepped onto the boardwalk. No glass in the windows, a thousand bullet holes in the walls and the swinging doors, but men still wanted to drink and play cards and talk to good-looking women.

It was nice, in a way, to see that some things never changed.

Although, as he stepped inside, The Kid saw the saloon wasn't nearly as busy as it sometimes was. In fact, Sophia spotted him right away and came over to him. She had changed her dress and cleaned the blood off her face. She had a bandage over the cut, put there no doubt by Dr. Eggars.

"Hello, Kid," she said with a smile. "I didn't expect to see you again so soon."

"I came into town to pick up a few supplies," he explained.

"Supplies? Where are you going?"

"I never intended to stay in Rattlesnake Valley. I was always just passing through."

Sophia frowned. "You're leaving tonight? But that's crazy! You could stay at Diamondback for a few days and rest up from everything that's happened."

"Diana suggested that," The Kid replied with a shake of his head, "but I figured it might be best if I rode on."

"Keep her from getting ideas in her head, huh?"

"Something like that."

"Well, you can have a drink before you get those supplies," Sophia said. "It's on the house."

"I already have the supplies," The Kid said. "I just stopped in here to say good-bye."

Her smile was shaken by that. "But . . . but . . . there's no reason for you to leave so fast. People around here owe you so much!"

"No, they don't," The Kid insisted. "I didn't do it for them. I became mixed up in this because I didn't like Malone, and then I found out that he and Parnell both had to be stopped. Somebody had to do it. It just happened to be me."

"You can believe that if you want to, Kid, but I don't. Fate brought you here."

The Kid leaned down and brushed his lips over her cheek. "Good-bye, Sophia." He turned and walked to the door, shouldering through the batwings.

She followed him onto the porch. "Kid," she said with a note of longing entering her voice as he swung up onto the buckskin, "Kid . . . you can stay here for a spell . . . if you want."

He paused and smiled down at her. "I reckon I do want that," he said, "and that's exactly the problem, right there."

With that he lifted the reins and turned the horse. His heels sent the buckskin into a trot that carried him toward the eastern edge of town, the rest of the valley, and the wasteland beyond.

He thought he heard Sophia call softly, "Kid!" behind him, but he couldn't be sure, and so he kept riding.